Finding Millions

Jason Garey

Contents

Chapter 1

W hen the first crack of a gunshot rang out across the valley, the city was asleep. Many would wake up in the morning to the news, and it would unnerve them to their core.

The dark-colored four-door pickup truck was aggressively accelerating and struggling to increase the distance between itself and a white SUV chasing it. As the truck approached a stop light, the driver pulled a hard right turn without slowing. With tires screaming and smoke pouring off the back, the truck tore a path across two lanes of the deserted city street. The scars of the aggressive move were left on the gray city streets for all to see. The SUV slowed to make the same turn, but it was now under the city lights and the lead vehicle's passengers could identify the vehicle chasing them as a white Suburban as it continued to pursue.

Just behind the Suburban, and unbeknownst to either vehicle, another automobile had been shadowing the lead car since the exchange occurred over an hour ago. It increased speed to keep up with the chase but remained a dozen car lengths behind the Suburban. This Ford Mustang was now passing under the bright city streetlights and was visible even though its headlights were turned off.

The car chase continued through the almost abandoned streets of this quiet little city in the rolling hills of East Tennessee.

The chase began when the F-150 had become alarmed when the Suburban had moved in too aggressively behind them. It had appeared from nowhere, and though it was late at night, the headlights seemed to come up from the side of the road. The F-150 made an unscheduled last second turn off the exit to see if it was being followed, and the Suburban took the bait. Then the first gunshot was an attempt to hit the tires. The driver quickly adjusted to a driving style that would be considered dangerous. Then the truck's rear cab windows were lowered as the men in the back seat began returning fire. All shots seemed to be missing both vehicles as their erratic driving made it difficult to aim.

At the next turn, the F-150 lost control as half the tires left the pavement and the other half hit the curb at high speed. The driver bounced high in the cab as he temporarily fought for control of the truck. A loud thud and then a crunching sound echoed off the street, and the truck spun in a half circle as it bounced across the sidewalk and barely missed a telephone poll. The Suburban aimed at the rear of the truck and increased speed. The truck regained control and the driver mashed down on the accelerator. It was a near miss. Both cars were now out of position and off the road. The truck was driving across a gas station parking lot. The Suburban was completely off-road in an empty lot and increasing speed to follow the truck. The truck left the bumpy gas station lot and made a hard left turn and started down Windy Hill Road. This twisting turning road was dark, and leaving the city streetlight gave the truck an opportunity to try to shake off the Suburban.

About five minutes away, Cal had just returned home after a long day, and he was ready for a beer. As he exited his Jeep in the driveway, he looked up at the bulbous white orb floating just above the dark outline of the mountains in the distance. The temperature was brisk for Tennessee, thirty-six degrees, and the sky was clear. This was the type of moon that captured your attention and made you feel small and insignificant in the universe. He stared for a long moment until his eyes burned from the brightness and a cold weather chill ran up his spine.

He opened the door and went into the kitchen, setting his takeout on the counter as he took a cold beer from the refrigerator and cracked it open. The fizzing sound was the only sound in the house. He took a big swallow, and then another. His dog Daisy looked up from her dog bed and studied him.

"Hey, girl, you miss me?"

She started to pop up, as if the magic word would be used. Treat. It was not.

He drank some more.

Cal was tired. He'd attended three sales meetings, which was more than typical, and he had driven over five hours total. It was now after ten thirty, and he was mad at himself for getting home so late.

He was exhausted and wanted to sit down and watch some college basketball. He was more than physically exhausted, but he had yet to realize how much his life and his choices weighed on his psyche.

He called Daisy over to the front door.

"Here, girl."

She sprang up from her dog bed and sprinted out the door with her hind legs sliding on the wooden front deck. She ran to her usual spot in the front yard and squatted. When she was done, she hustled back to the open door and returned to her plush dog bed.

Cal walked over to the white and gray granite counter top and opened the thin, white takeout bag. The translucent bag all restaurants seemed to use appeared to stick to the black foam takeout container. It made its customary crunching sounds of discomfort as he wiggled it loose. Inside he found his favorite Thai food dish. He grabbed a fork from the drawer, turned, and went into the small, beige-carpeted living room.

With his Pad Thai and fork in one hand and his beer in the other, he headed to his favorite brown chair. A chair you could watch television, host guests, or easily fall asleep in at night.

He set down both of his items on the small, wood-grain TV stand next to the chair. He turned and faced the front window. He picked up the beer and stared out at the full moon.

He was glad to be home and even happier it was the weekend. He had a job, but it was going nowhere. He would work and save and work and save until the job disappeared or a better one came along. He reflected on his mediocrity for a moment and then on his day. This was his life, for better or worse.

He took another sip.

It was sometimes nice to be single. His mind was open to quiet time and reflection. Sometimes he was able to grab and hold onto a moment in time, such as this one. There were no outside influences or plans or schedules to distract him. He could deeply appreciate a beautiful moment without having to call someone over to take a picture to share on social media. He genuinely appreciated the beauty of the moment and felt better for it.

His dog rubbed against the side of his leg. She also stared out the window.

Daisy's ears perked up and she put her paws on the windowsill.

"Hey, Daisy," he said. "What's up, girl?"

She stared out the window with her ears high. He went over to the wall and turned off the inside lights and watched the yard and the road beyond with zero reflection, and due to the brightness of the moon, he could see the entire front yard, even out to the main road.

He saw nothing, so he waited and listened.

Cal was staring out the window and watching the full moon when he heard the sound as it echoed off the hills around him. Gunshots were uncommon around his home. Although he was not necessarily living in the country, it had been considered rural farmland about twenty years ago. The house was not near anyone and was surrounded by fields and farms. However, just down the road was a series of newer housing developments, older homes, and older farms.

He heard it again, but this time the gunshot sounded closer. The third, fourth, and fifth shot rang out in rapid succession. Now Cal could see two sets of headlights heading toward his land. They were moving more rapidly than the road was designed for. The trailing car even swerved dangerously off the blacktop with the headlights disappearing for a few seconds. The lead car did not slow down but instead gained distance between the vehicles and increased its speed as it crested the hill. The rear car was now out of view as the lead car approached Cal's driveway. As it approached his land and a grove of pine trees, Cal could see two large bags being thrown out of the truck's passenger side windows. They carried over the drainage ditch and landed in the thick pine needles at the base of some large old pine trees.

Cal could see the vehicle clearly now. It was not a car at all, but a Ford pickup truck.

The trailing car passed by his drive about ten seconds later and was increasing speed as well. It crested the hill in front of his house and was gone in a moment. The taillights were darting across the road as it gained on the F-150, and then, they were gone. Out of sight.

Cal was standing there staring down the road, waiting for sirens or more car lights. He thought about the bags and how it was perfect timing to ditch the bags. No one following would be able to see the bags leaving the truck after they crested the hill.

After a moment, he grabbed his beer and lifted it to his lips. Taking a large sip, he turned his head and looked toward the road in the distance.

Did he really just see a car chase?

"Wow, girl, did you see that?" he asked Daisy.

Another car went by his drive at high speed.

"What is going on tonight?" he said aloud.

A final crack of a gun in the distance was the last one he heard.

He was wondering what was happening to his quiet road when he found himself focusing on the pine grove. It was dark under the trees, and he could not make out the bags clearly.

Gunshots and car chases. However, no police. No sirens. What was this all about?

His first tendency was to run up to the road and check out those bags. However, his rational brain kicked in. Obviously, unless it was trash, these guys with the guns were coming back. The last thing he wanted was to be up there by the road when they made their way back to his little piece of countryside.

He would let it sit there awhile and watch what might happen.

His food was getting cold, but he had no interest in food right now. He was enthralled with the excitement of what just occurred.

He paced in front of the window for twenty minutes, eyes fixated on the road. A car or two had passed by, but no one had even slowed down near his driveway.

He had finished the first beer a few minutes ago and was now opening his second. Soon he had built up enough courage to put his shoes and coat back on. His mind was swimming in ideas of what the bags contained. Money, guns, drugs, diamonds, or something completely awful. It was worth a look, any excitement would be worth it, and if it was valuable, all the better. Cal was craving excitement, and anything involving gunshots and a car chase was worth it.

He went back to the window. Wanting to be sure, he waited another ten minutes. These guys were sure being slow about it. What if it was trash? Why the shootout?

"Daisy, are you ready for my theory? These guys are throwing trash on people's lawns, until one night they picked the wrong house, and a grumpy old man saw what happened. He jumped in his car and started chasing them. Then they exchanged gunfire?"

Daisy looked up at him with a questioning look. Scratch that idea. He had to know. The suspense was too much for him, and he took a long look in each direction of the road. Nothing. No cars.

He grabbed a flashlight out of the kitchen drawer and headed to the door. He turned off all the lights and gave Daisy a whistle. She came running out of the door.

He approached the pine grove alone. Daisy was not allowed near the road, and she knew it. He was cautious and kept his eye looking toward the distant road. The last thing he wanted was to be surprised by a car.

He looked at Daisy, the white Labrador retriever, and she was in her usual spot sniffing and circling the ground. She was, any minute now, going to do her business. She was the best pet for a single guy such as Cal. She was obedient and loyal, a true companion, and she could hold her bowels for long periods of time. Most importantly, she would let anyone pet and rub her belly, which was great for meeting women at the park or on a hiking trail.

She found her spot and squatted in the yard.

Cal turned his attention back toward the pine grove with his flashlight shining. He spotted two bags lying in a bed of pine needles. He walked up to the first bag. He switched his flashlight from his right hand to his left. Then he sneaked one more look down the road in either direction. No cars, no headlights, no sound, but he needed to hurry.

He bent down and inspected the outside of the first bag. It was long and rectangular shaped. Cal ran his hand over the outside of what looked like nylon, and it reminded him of some military surplus equipment. The bag was worn and coarse to the touch. He felt around and searched for the zipper, finding it along the left side. He placed the flashlight in his mouth and rolled the bag over, pulling it toward himself. It was heavy, heavier than it looked like it should be. He opened the bag and the light in his mouth entered the gap in the bag. Inside he saw green, lots and lots of green. Stacks of green. One-hundred-dollar bills filled the bag to its capacity.

Cal's mind skipped a beat, and he blinked hard and looked again. As the blood and adrenaline rushed to his head, he felt weak in the legs and his fight or flight mechanism had just activated.

Cal's heart was pounding now. Sweat was pouring off his brow and his arms were tingling. A flood of fight or flight sensations were overtaking him. He had not felt like this since his last speeding ticket.

This was the kind of money one only sees in a gangster movie. The average person will never see such a haul, and Cal was an average guy. He was not ready for this.

He felt his heart rate increasing and the slight pressure on his skull. After a moment, a slight dizziness began to creep in. Cal dropped to both knees and started moving his hands around the inside of the bag. It was full and packed tight.

He looked around furiously. He was sure this was not real and must be counterfeit money.

"Woah." Cal let out a sigh.

How could this happen? This never happened to anyone.

He zipped up the bag and looked around and then repeated the process on the second bag, same result. Money, nothing but stacks of big bills could be seen.

Cal felt even more strange. His heart rate had increased for sure. He also had a nice little buzz going from drinking beers on an empty stomach.

There was a new feeling growing inside him. It was rising from his stomach and growing with intensity. Greed. He felt like he needed to protect this money. He needed to get it out of sight and into his house.

He was convincing himself of this when Daisy's ears popped up and she started a low growl. She pointed her nose to the trees across the road. Cal switched off the light and felt for the zipper. When he found it, he zipped the second bag closed. The dog's head dipped low and her posture changed. Cal looked around and saw nothing, so he pushed the button on the flashlight and shined the light into the trees across the road. There he saw a pair of red eyes about halfway up a tree.

"It's OK, girl." He spoke softly. "It's all good. Let's go inside."

Cal bent down and hoisted the heavy bag on his shoulder. He guessed around twenty pounds.

"What the hell?" he said. "Who would ever throw this much money away?"

He walked down the hill.

Daisy ran up to him.

"Daisy girl, you wouldn't throw this away, would you? No, you wouldn't," he said shaking his head.

The two of them walked back down to the garage. Cal punched his code on the keypad. One, nine, seven, seven. The door started to open, and Daisy rushed under the garage door and stood by the door leading to the kitchen. He walked over and opened the house door to let Daisy inside. He turned and dropped the large duffel bag and headed back up the hill to retrieve the second bag. A few moments later, he pressed the button to close the garage door.

He dropped everything on the concrete garage floor. Cal stood over them and stared. He was nervous to see his treasure in the pure light. Maybe his mind was playing tricks on him before. He hovered over it for a moment and then opened both bags and dumped the contents on the floor. He searched for any signs of who may have owned them. He ran his hands down the seams and found nothing. There had been nothing in the bag except stacks of money.

He pushed the two black bags aside and started counting the money. He started stacking the ten-thousand-dollar bound greenbacks into one-hundred-thousand-dollar stacks. Ten high. He then began pushing all the piles close together so they were all level. The garage floor was filling up with stacks of cash all in a neat row and all the same height.

Cal counted piles, twenty-two.

"Whoa!" he exclaimed. That was two hundred twenty ten-thousand-dollar bundles. That was two point two million dollars.

"This is almost too much money," he exclaimed again. The type of people who had this kind of money did not leave it along a country road. He remembered the gunshots and the other car chasing the truck. They were obviously in trouble and trying to hide it in his trees.

"But for how long?" he questioned out loud.

Now the thoughts in his head were less about protecting the money and more about protecting himself. He never thought there would be so much money just thrown away. He did not know what to expect before checking the bags, but he thought possibly drugs, guns, or even something completely random like old tools or a porn collection were stashed in them. No way did he expect the forty-five pounds of cash sitting on his garage floor.

His mind was racing. What did he do now? This amount of money and being involved with the people who kept this quantity of cash could be dangerous for him.

However, he really wanted to keep the money. He needed to decide, and quickly, before someone came back for it.

Chapter 2

C al could hear a vehicle coming down the road. He was getting more nervous with each passing minute.

"Where to hide it?" he said aloud. "Where?"

Men with guns might show up in his front yard at any moment. He needed to make sure there was no trace of it in his garage. There needed to be some real distance between himself and the money.

Would they kill him if they believed he found it? There had already been gunshots. Or would they even remember where they tossed it?

He started to repack the bags carefully so all the money would fit back in.

He was almost positive the bags contained no tracking devices. However, he had to be sure. He checked every corner again and felt the entire canvas bag for any bulge or raised area. There was none. If there had been a tracker, they would have seen the move to the garage anyway. He decided to use the bags again. He needed to be covert; the black bags were sturdy and camouflaged for the darkness outside.

When he finished, he closed the bags and went inside to change into hiking clothes and boots.

He went into his bedroom and sat on his bed for a moment. He looked over and caught himself staring at the clock. His head was starting to clear, but the adrenaline was starting to wear off and making him feel a little nauseous.

A few minutes had passed, and Cal knew he was wasting valuable time. He stood and walked over to the dresser and started hurriedly pulling out some warm clothes.

When he came back to the money, he was wearing a black hoodie, black pants with hiking boots, and was holding a flashlight. All to blend into the night.

The clock was ticking now, and the urge to run was overwhelming. Should he just get in his Jeep and drive? Just go. Anywhere.

He lifted both bags on his back and crossed the straps to keep them secure, pushed the garage door button, and headed out into the darkness, closing the door behind him with the keypad.

His house was completely dark now, and the only sounds inside would come from Daisy barking if anyone came close.

Cal was a regional sales manager for a kitchen supply company which worked with restaurants and fast-food chains. He sold ovens, refrigerators, microwaves, and other kitchen equipment along with the supplies and maintenance plans. He was not a ninja or a spy, so he felt a little out of his depth.

Cal walked across his yard in the darkness with the light of the radiant full moon shining down on his hiking boots and the long, carefully mowed backyard. He stepped over flowerbeds and garden hoses. Everything was gray and shadow, but he knew where he was going. It would take about twenty minutes to get to his destination in the sunlight, but this may take a little bit longer. At the edge of his property, he crossed over the sunken chain-link fence. It had dipped into the ground over the countless years of gardening and farming next to it.

From this point on, the grass was taller as he entered the hayfield, and it started grabbing at his feet. He kept up a steady pace going directly east and hoping and praying that no one had seen him leave.

He had left Daisy in the house just to be sure that no one would see or notice him or hear her barking. He needed to be as stealthy as possible on the way there and back again.

He headed down the hill through the hayfields behind his house. The moon was luminous, and he did not really need the flashlight for this part of the journey. He crossed a large part of open land after he left his property and followed the moonlight deep into the hayfields.

He eventually made it to a large spring in the field and crossed a little creek that trickled out and down, eventually meeting a large stream about a quarter mile away. The mud was thick here, and he struggled a little bit with all the extra weight on his back. He was sweating now and was ready for a break, but he kept moving on. He was overcome by the need to get the money to a safe location.

He was halfway toward his goal.

The high grass was now cleaning the mud off his boots and legs. This was not a smooth walk. There were dips and holes and tall grass that caught his feet. The landscape from his deck looked like a smooth sloping field, but from where he was, it was anything but smooth.

He brushed his arm against his brow to wipe the sweat off.

Then he turned and looked at his house. No lights, no cars, and everything looked fine. Even though his home looked small in the distance, he knew exactly how far he had come.

He had been walking for a while. He knew the field was just over a hundred acres to the next fence, and he was almost there now.

He pushed on. There were trees along the fence line, and their darkness loomed just ahead of him now. He walked up to the dark shade of a tree and dropped to his knees. He took the bags off and rested.

After a couple minutes, Cal got up off the ground and started looking for a gap in the old fence line. He knew there were several down here, but at night it was hard to see.

Cal needed his flashlight but was fearful someone might see it. He took a long look around to make sure he could not see anything or anyone. He felt it was safe.

He grabbed the flashlight from his pocket and shined it along the fence line looking for a place in the barbed wire where it had been cut many years ago.

He spotted a gap. It was right next to a little leaning tree. He walked back and picked up the bags, got them situated on his back, and headed toward the leaning tree.

It was almost midnight now, and Cal had moved into the tree line. He was no longer visible from the road, which was a long way away and up the hill.

He was almost there. The goal of his journey was just ahead of him.

Then he saw his destination.

At one time, an old farmhouse and barn stood on this part of the property. The house had fallen in on itself back in the early nineties during a March blizzard. There was no real loss as this house had not been occupied since the nineteen fifties.

Cal often walked down to this part of the property in good fall or spring weather. He had explored the barn and house remains many times. No one came down here, ever. The old driveway was now covered in trees and there was no access. The only way into this little cove was through the fence row, and it was lined with trees and dense ground cover. Blackberries and old grape vines lined the row as well. It was truly the best hiding space he could think of. It was close, yet not accessible. The only person who ever tread near this area was the old farmer from down the road. He cut the hayfield several times a year, loaded the six-foot round bales, and left. He was not interested in anything but the hay and avoiding the heat. He often cut, raked, and baled hay early in the morning.

Cal came out of the trees and saw what was left of the old hay barn. Only one corner of the structure could be seen. It had two walls creating a right angle, proof of human intention to settle here. The rest of the barn had collapsed. Pieces of itself were stacked in the middle of the foundation. It looked as if the heavy rains of the fall had collapsed the remaining structure even more than the last time he'd seen it.

He started walking around the barn. It was overgrown with bushes, grass, and small trees. The debris of the several different collapses were strewn out in front of him.

He shone the flashlight around until he found his target. The old claw-foot porcelain tub was sitting on its side. It was directly under the section of barn still standing. He headed for the old tub.

He was sweating heavily now. The journey was a good hike, but the heavy and awkward bags had made the trip grueling.

He reached the tub and set both bags on the ground. He reached into his front pocket and pulled out two black garbage bags.

Cal's intention was to add a layer of camouflage and protection to the money. No one would want to open old garbage bags. However, if they saw black nylon bags, who would not open those? Cal also thought the weather could damage the money and thought the plastic would help protect it.

He unfolded the garbage bags as big as he could, snapping them in the night air and opening them fully. He managed to get each money bag to fit into its own extra-large yard bag. He tied off the top of the first bag. At least no one would suspect these bags of holding cash, and it would help protect them against the weather.

He reached into the other garbage bag and unzipped the money bag. He pulled out six stacks of cash and put them in his pocket. Then he zipped the money bag closed and secured the top of the garbage bag. He moved the garbage bags over next to the claw-foot tub.

With all his effort, he pulled, leaned, and grunted. The tub then gave way and turned over, landing on top of the bags.

Cal started shining his light around and found several old boards. He walked over and started throwing them on top of the tub. It looked natural. He surveyed his hiding spot and felt good that nothing could be seen, even if you were looking for it.

On the way back he thought of everything from kids stumbling across the money to rats or mice eating it. Maybe he should bring some moth balls back tomorrow. No, he could not come back until he was sure it was safe. He needed a real plan first and a good way to move the money.

As he carefully walked toward his home in the darkness, he kept a watchful eye for anything out of the ordinary.

He saw nothing.

When he finally reached his house, he was exhausted. He sat in a lawn chair on his front porch and stared at the empty road. He was staring at the road in the cool night air for a while when he fell asleep.

Cal snapped up and looked around about twenty minutes later. He was remembering his adventure and searching for anything out of place. How could he fall asleep out here? Was he stupid? He went inside.

He stripped off his clothes, threw them in the washing machine, and spread out on the couch.

He did not want to sleep. He wanted to rest for a moment. Thinking was more important. He wanted to know about the men shooting at each other. He wanted to know his adversary because he was keeping this money, but sleep overtook him against his wishes.

As he drifted in and out of sleep, he decided to go to his bed.

Chapter 3

L uis González, aka Rooftop, was waiting for his men, or at least a phone call from one of them. He had three teams out on the streets looking for his lost crew, the money, or answers.

Crew number four, his best soldiers led by a longtime friend, had made the exchange over four hours ago. They reported in initially. No problems. Cocaine for the cash. They had the money and were on their way back. Something was wrong.

An hour ago, fearing something more sinister, he had called in all his most trusted men. They were all waiting in the CK Hot Rods and Auto Garage on the east side. One of the semi-legitimate businesses the gang controlled, Luis owned, and where the rise to the top of the organization had started for him. This was the place he used for an impressive victory over a rival gang nearly twenty years before.

His second-in-command, Jimmy, was with him, in addition to their usual entourage. The room was filling up, and that was hard to do.

The back room of the garage was large; it had been an addition added by the early owners of this place. Most likely in the 1950s. It was designed to be a storage room for tires and other auto parts. It was huge, nearly two thousand square feet. It was an open room with light wood paneling on the walls. Concrete floors and shop lighting hung from a tall open ceiling. Around the outside were signs and bar lights from closed and abandoned bars from all over the city.

There was a full bar, four couches, two televisions, and even three refrigerators in a small kitchen.

In the middle there were three long tables and chairs set up for the crews to eat. In the corner was an office, Luis' natural wood desk, nice leather chairs, and some bookshelves. It was arranged where he could look out over the whole room.

Luis had used this as his personal office for almost fifteen years now. He bought the place when he was just sixteen years old. It had been abandoned, and the neighborhood was nearly vacant except for the drug trafficking, which he oversaw.

"Jimmy, have Jesús keep calling these guys. Try all their phones. I want an answer soon."

"You got it, Boss," Jimmy said.

Jimmy walked across the room to his number two guy and gave him his instructions.

The key to a good organization was always a strong pyramid. Jimmy had passed this nugget of information to Luis when he was just an initiate. Luis had taken it to heart. Every officer and leader in the organization had to declare a number two, and they had to be trained in all aspects of their bosses' job and theirs. If ever any foul play was involved to move up the ranks, justice would be swift. All moves up were earned, not taken.

And so, they waited. For a couple hours the members drank coffee, talked, and watched television. Luis was tired of waiting for his crew to call, and he was now convinced that call would never come.

"Juan, over here," Luis yelled.

"Yeah, Boss," came the reply.

"Get your crew together and get up to that casino. Check out the area, level four stairway on the far side of the garage away from the elevators. Make sure nothing happened there. Call me after you have checked it out. But stay there in case the Russians show up."

"On it, Boss," came the confident reply. Being called into action out of a whole room showed how much respect Luis had for Juan and his crew. Everyone knew it, and they all felt it.

Juan's crew headed to the gun room and presented themselves to the quartermaster.

The quartermaster looked at Luis. Luis gave him a nod.

Then the quartermaster and Juan gave each other a forearm locking embrace. These old friends did this every time one of them went out on a mission.

The four-man crew were each issued a handgun in a shoulder holster for under their coats, and one man was issued an MP5 sub machine gun with three clips.

This type of organization was necessary to keep his gang out of trouble and from making simple mistakes. The quartermaster controlled the weapons and had a count of everything. He had five stashes of weapons hidden around their territory, and only Luis and the quartermaster, whose name was Jose but who'd been called Glock since Luis gave him that name during the Crazy Eddie incident, knew where it all was. This secrecy was the one exception to the rule of number twos knowing everything. There was no number two for the quartermaster role. It was one of secrecy and trust. If you got this position, you knew too much. You had to be trustworthy.

Guns and drugs and money all passed through Glock's fingers. He was smart and cunning and completely loyal to Luis and the gang. At thirty-four years old, Glock had been with Luis since he was an initiate.

There were six men at the top of the pyramid with Luis being at the very top. Below him were five others. Jimmy, Priest, Juan, Glock, and Pedro. These were the original Little TSGs. The stories told about them were legendary.

A sentry squawked over the radio. "We got a crew coming in."

Jimmy hustled back over to Luis' desk.

The men stared at the radio on the desk.

A minute passed.

"Pedro's crew are headed in."

"Copy," came the reply from the front door.

The heavy metal reinforced door was unlocked, and the men entered the room.

"Something's wrong," mumbled Jimmy.

"I know," whispered Luis.

Pedro left his men at the bar and came to report to Luis.

"Boss, the sun was coming up, we had to get out of there," said Pedro.

"You afraid of the sun or the cops?" asked Luis. "Get your guys back on the street. I want a show of force. Keep the weapons on you."

"You got it, Boss," came the reply. "You expect trouble?"

"Yes!"

Jimmy interjected, "This did not go down the way it was supposed to. We have worked with these guys several times before, but this was a big exchange. We don't know what to expect. Be ready."

"Yeah, Jimmy, we'll be ready," Pedro replied. He looked at Jimmy's belt. "You should be carrying tonight, Jimmy, might be worse than we thought."

Pedro patted Jimmy on the back and went to instruct his men and let the quartermaster know. The quartermaster gave Pedro a slap on the back and they locked arms.

"Jimmy, we need more information," demanded Luis.

"Agreed, but the damn drop is an hour and a half from here, and very public," Jimmy responded. "That was the point."

"Any news from the casino area?" Luis yelled to his guys watching TV.

"No, Boss, we are checking."

"It's 6:30 now," Jimmy started. "We need to reach out to the Russians. They may know what happened."

"The Russian leadership wants our business, really, they need us right now, and we want it too," sighed Luis. "No, this is something else."

"If the boys got busted, they will never break," Jimmy responded. "I doubt they would get picked up. My guess is someone hit them after their call in."

"Our boys will be dead, not busted, not worried about that," Luis replied. "I'm worried that someone knows too much about our operations. We have loose lips, or we are being watched."

They both paused and took that information in. Both never would consider a mole in their operation. This was a family, but a ruthless one. They all understood what would happen if they talked.

"Any word on Julio?" asked Luis.

Jimmy looked up with concern. "No, his mom and his girl have not seen him in two weeks. What was he doing when he went missing?"

"I had him running some messages to Atlanta and then doing some recon on the casino parking garage."

"I'm guessing he knew the details?" asked Jimmy.

"He knows enough. He even ran shipments to the storage locker."

Jimmy looked more concerned. He asked, "Did we check the locker?"

"It's safe," Luis confirmed.

"He's been with us for over ten years," said Jimmy. "I know he is a head case, but sell us out? No. He's got at least three kills and has no leverage with the cops. They get their fat fingers on him, and he's going down."

"We're watching the girlfriend's house and his mom's," Jimmy whispered. "I'll check in with the boys over there."

"Good, I have a bad feeling."

"Boss, take a look at this," one of his young members yelled from across the room. He had shared his phone with the TV.

"What is it?" Jimmy asked.

"Boss needs to see this," he replied.

"Let's take a look," Luis yelled.

On the screen was a news report from a local paper about forty minutes away in Springdale.

The headline read, "Gang Shootout at Springdale Marina."

"Jimmy, read that out loud."

Jimmy walked closer to the screen. He cleared his throat and began, "A shootout in the early hours of Saturday morning left eight men dead and no clear reason for the shooting. We also have numerous reports of a long car chase and shootout along Windy Hill Road at the same time. Police speculate the men were both part of rival gangs in the Knoxville area and not local to Springdale. The FBI is on scene and gathering evidence. Several weapons have been found, and it appears that all assailants died at the scene.

"We will update you with the latest. Subscribe here for blah blah…"

"Luis, Jimmy, I need you for a minute," came a call from Glock.

"Hey, Luis, I don't have enough weapons here to arm everyone. I'm short. We just lost six guns in that shootout, and they are not coming back."

"OK, OK, keep your voice down. Right now, keep your Glock on you, one for that new kid assistant, put him over the cage, and you go get a refill."

"You got it," Glock said.

"You need any help?"

"Naw, we should keep the location to ourselves right now."

Glock reached in his back belt and pulled out a Glock forty caliber and handed it to Luis. "Just in case."

Luis nodded.

"Oh, and Pedro is going to crossbar the steel doors, we don't want any surprises."

"Good thinking," Jimmy said with a smirk. "Never know what could happen, the Russians could send five teenagers after us."

They laughed as they separated.

"Good," came the reply. "I need to talk to the guys and then we need to get some more answers. Jimmy, you find me a lone target. I want the information direct, no rumors, I will take it from his bloody mouth, understood?"

"Yes, Boss," came the reply.

Luis walked over to a young soldier, whispered in his ear, and then walked over to the bar.

"The boss has something to say!" came a loud voice from the corner. All the televisions went off and the talking ceased. All eyes moved to the corner, and it was completely silent for twenty seconds as Luis made his way to the center of the room.

"Crew, it looks like we lost some of our family last night. Good men who were working for all our benefit. Now, they are gone. We will miss them. We are going to their homes when we know for sure. I want to see every member paying respect, no exceptions. We are a family and we stick together. But first, Priest, please pray for our fallen soldiers."

The men bowed their heads reverently.

Priest was covered head to toe in ink. He walked to the center of the room. Crossed himself and began.

"O God, by whose mercy the faithful departed find rest, look kindly on your departed soldiers who gave their lives in the service of their family. Grant that through the passion, death, and resurrection of your Son they may share in the joy of your heavenly kingdom and rejoice in you with your saints forever. Dear Lord Jesus and Mary, Mother of God, hold all these remaining brave souls in the palm of your hand, comfort them and their families. Send angels of protection, love, and comfort to all the crew still at war, bring them home safely and comfort their families. We ask this through Christ our Lord. Amen."

"Amen!"

All the men crossed themselves and stared at Luis for what came next.

"Jimmy, read the list and surviving family," Luis said.

Jimmy pulled a small book from his pocket. Inside, written with a special code, was a list of the crew, their specialties, family, and any other information Jimmy kept, including rank and seniority. It was in a made-up code and only Jimmy could read it. He began to read from the list.

"Crew four:

"Jose Martinez, full member, survived by his mom Roberta and sister Mia.

"Juan Carlos Ruiz, officer, no family but his crew.

"Antonio Rodriguez, full member, survived by his sister Carla.

"Angel Moreno, initiate, no family but his crew.

"These were our brothers and their family are our family. We will light candles for them tonight at St. Augustus. We will begin mourning with their families tomorrow, black bands on the left arm."

Luis raised his head slowly and spoke. "Now, going forward, no one in this gang goes anywhere without their crew. All men will be armed except initiates. Initiates, this is a learning experience, stay close to your crew and learn from them. That is your job. Crew officers, keep your crew safe. We are not standing and fighting. We are getting information. When we know more, we will bury those responsible for this and their families. Understood?"

They nodded, acknowledging their boss.

Luis walked over to Priest. He lowered his voice. "Priest, call in some breakfast and coffee for everyone, we are going to be here for a while."

Priest nodded his head and went over to the bar to make a call.

Priest was Luis' bodyguard and ran his HQ. He oversaw food, the bar, cash, payoffs to cops, and anything else that came in the door. He could get anything they needed. He didn't like to get his hands dirty anymore, since he had re-committed himself to Christ. Prison and being shot were big motivators to the faith.

Priest, Ricardo Sanchez, was invaluable to Luis. He had run crews and knew the streets. He was a soldier and a leader. Many years ago, he had been in a shootout with a rival gang and been shot in the stomach, a near miss. The real troubles came when the cops arrived and found an unlicensed and thus illegal MAC-10, capable of firing twelve hundred nine-millimeter rounds per minute, lying next to a wounded Priest.

Luis' defense lawyer got Priest off on all other charges claiming self-defense, but the weapons charge stood. He was sentenced to five years. He was out in three.

During his time, he never said one word to anyone in the hospital, jail, or the courthouse. In prison, he only spoke with TSG or affiliates. The only person he ever spoke with outside of TSG was his attorney, who Luis had told him to trust. His silence and the fact that communication was only one-way earned him the name. It's like confession. He'd just nod at you. The joke name of Priest was issued. When he became devout, it stuck.

Priest was sincere and deliberate. His advice was only given when he knew for sure the facts were in his favor.

As a bodyguard, he was intimidating and deadly. He was also fiercely loyal to Luis and Jimmy.

Priest was an original Little TSG. He had been with Luis since they'd started and had been to war many times. Priest always carried a gun and did the driving, security, and logistics for Luis and the gang. He knew how to hit the enemy and came up with the most creative tactics, so he was the best at preventing attacks as well.

"Keep your eyes out, that goes for everyone," Luis yelled. "I mean it. The appearance of weakness may provoke our enemies to attack. We are far from weak, but we will not be taken by surprise."

"Yeah, Boss," came the reply.

Luis and Jimmy walked back to the office area.

Jimmy looked at him for a long moment. "What now?"

"Now we talk to the Russians, and we get some answers, or revenge."

Chapter 4

Officer Collins took an enormous risk in obtaining this information. Earlier that month, Collins had pulled over a gang member, most likely from Atlanta, and had gotten lucky. This kid talked and talked, anything to try to avoid life in jail.

Collins had been working an afternoon shift when he noticed a tattoo-covered driver in a classic Impala with flames on the side. When the driver passed, he got a good look. He recognized the distinctive TSG tattoo on the driver's left arm and knew they had no business in Springdale. That was a big city problem. He was going to put a stop to any gang presence in his town, so he would follow him, and if he got the opportunity, he would make an example out of him.

Collins pulled his unmarked police car out of the gas station parking lot and slowly followed the Impala through town. He ran his plates and checked for warrants. This guy had them all, and at nineteen years old, he was going to jail for a long time. His name was Julio Martinez, and he was wanted for murder, attempted murder, drug trafficking, and other assorted nonsense. His most recent warrants were for a shooting in Knoxville three months ago, and he was a prime suspect with his prints being found on a shell casing.

Collins was trailing Julio through a neighborhood street that started with houses but eventually turned into hayfields and then nothingness. The mountains in front of him offered little escape, and Collins knew he had nowhere to go, but he kept driving away from town.

This guy was acting way too nervous and driving down a farm road that would eventually end in the state forest. Once he was past the last of the housing developments, he sped up to catch the Impala. He went through some forested areas and then past a couple farms. When he did get behind the Impala, he stayed on his bumper till he made it past most of the houses. Nothing but logging trucks came down this road anymore. He followed him for the next mile and then turned on the lights.

Collins was the senior most officer in the Springdale Police Department. He had been there for twenty-one years. He was comfortable in his job, his earnings, his extra pay, and his side gig with the mayor. He had no plans of leaving anytime soon.

Collins owned a boat, RV, four-wheelers, a newer truck, and a nice country house with land. His three kids went to the private schools in town, and his wife was able to quit working about ten years ago. She had been an elementary school teacher.

Collins knew what he was doing. He did not call for backup, and he did not want any right now. The Chevy pulled over onto a grass shoulder next to a cattle fence, shut off the engine, and the driver stuck his hands out of the window.

Collins jumped out of the car with his weapon out and yelled for the driver to open the car door from the outside and slowly get out of the vehicle. Julio complied. He told him to lay on the ground with his hands stretched out.

Julio complied.

He asked him if he had any weapons or drugs. Julio said, "No, sir."

This was not your typical gangbanger going out in a blaze of glory. Julio was acting in the correct manner and complying with all instructions. Collins grabbed his hands and handcuffed them behind his back, stood him up, and brought him around to the trunk of the car. He searched him and found only a wad of cash, cigarettes, a lighter, and his wallet. He placed them on the trunk of the Impala and asked Julio, "What the hell are you doing in my town?"

"Just heading home, gonna visit my girl," Julio whispered.

Collins took Julio's ID out of his wallet. A Tennessee driver's license, Julio Martinez.

"Hello, Julio, do you know you have multiple warrants for your arrest?" asked Collins.

"No, sir," Julio said. "I have been out of town."

"Well, Julio, looks like you will be doing twenty to life, my friend," said Collins. "They have your prints at a murder scene."

"Naw, man, wasn't me," said Julio. "Wasn't me."

"No problem, tell it to the jury. I'm sure they will believe you when forensics shows the evidence of your fingerprint on a bullet casing that killed another gangbanger just like you."

Julio started to get angry. "I can't go down for that, man, I can't. My girl is pregnant, yo, and he drew on me first. It was self-defense, I swear. I was lucky to get out of there," Julio cried out.

"Not my choice, tell your lawyer."

"I can't go to the station, I'll never get out again," Julio responded.

Julio was starting to show symptoms of being high, and Collins was noticing. He had some skin sores visible on his arms. His pupils were dilated, and he was twitching his head to the left too frequently.

"What are you on?" Collins asked.

Julio looked up at him, and an idea popped into his head. A possible way to get out of this, or at least get a sentence reduction if this local didn't go for it.

"Just a little crank, no biggie."

"Oh, just a little crank."

Collins picked him up and pushed him into the rear of the car.

"Let's see what they think of you in the can tonight."

"Nah, man, it just some dope, no biggie."

Collins slapped him across the face.

"Whoa, man, why you hit me?"

"Oh, did you feel that?"

Collins smacked him again.

Julio charged into Collins, knocking him backward on his hood.

Collins pulled his gun and smacked Julio across the face with it.

Julio dropped to his knees. "Ah my God, you crazy!"

"Stay there," yelled Collins. "Forget the can, you can go in the dirt instead."

"Nah, man, you crazy, you can't do that."

"I can't?" asked Collins. "This is my town, I will bury you in my backyard if I want to."

Collins walked up and kicked Julio in the side, and he fell on the gravel road. Collins began kicking him again and again.

"Stop, man," Julio cried out. "You're a cop."

"You picked the wrong town, banger," exclaimed Collins. "This is it for you."

He walked over and placed the gun against Julio's head.

"What do you want, cop?"

"Nothing, punk, you are not going to be missed. You have warrants and I am saving the taxpayers a lot of money. Locking you up would be a vacation for you."

"What if I gave you some good info, would you let me go?"

"Info?" Collins started laughing. "What kind of info?" asked Collins.

"There is a big deal going down, lots of cash and drugs, more than any of us have ever seen," said Julio, rising slowly to his knees.

"Yeah, big and bogus, my friend, you would say anything to live," said Collins.

Julio tried to fall to the gravel ground to beg, but Collins caught him and stood him upright.

"Naw, man, I swear. We have a deal going down with the Russians. They need a large amount of product for a shipment to Canada or someplace, and we have it from a big deal with the Mexican cartel last month. It's huge. The Russian suppliers got busted, so we are getting a great price to be rid of it. They will make a hundred times over. For us, it would take us all year to sell it."

"Where and when is this deal going down?" asked Collins.

"What are you gonna do for me?" asked Julio.

"I can walk away, but you have to go back to wherever you were hiding," said Collins.

"No problem, man, you got it, anything," said Julio.

Collins stared at this fool. Was this doped up hood telling the truth? This was big news and could be worth a fortune.

"Tell me about it."

Julio paused and just stared at Collins.

"Well?"

Julio was thinking about his crew and how he was betraying them. Then Collins struck him in the mouth with the butt of his gun.

Julio cried out. "Shit, man. They will kill me if they find out it was me. These are my boys."

"I will kill you right now if you don't tell me," explained Collins.

Collins hit him in the stomach, and Julio bent over in pain.

Julio began coughing and gasping for breath.

"It's in storage unit B322 at Storage Barn on Winchester Road, near the airport. Check it out. It's inside the stove."

"Where is the cash exchange?" asked Collins.

"The big Indian casino parking garage next Tuesday night at 8:30, fourth level near the stairs, east side."

"Come over here to the side of the car," said Collins. "Tell me again, start from the beginning."

Collins sat Julio down in the grass beside the car, and Julio repeated the story word for word.

It was very convincing, and Collins had made up his mind.

Collins thought this could all be made up to get a cop like himself to let him go, but the details were too precise. He had been looking around for a few minutes and saw no one out here during that whole time. He felt comfortable out here on the edge of the forest, so he bent down, grabbed his throwaway gun out of his ankle holster, and shot Julio in the head.

He returned the gun to its holster and walked over and dragged Julio's body down into the drainage ditch next to the cattle fence. He went to his car, grabbed a tarp out of the trunk, and covered the body. He placed a few small rocks on the edges to hold it down and got on his phone to call Denny. Denny was off today, but he would come and help him clean this up. He would bring his truck, and they would move the body to a place in the state forest. He told Denny he had hit a 10-point deer. The code word had been given, and Denny would bring the garbage bags, lye, shovels, and the car carrier. He texted Denny the location, and twenty-eight minutes later Denny showed up.

They went to the ditch and rolled the body in the tarp, lowered the tailgate on the truck, and lifted the body up and out of the ditch and onto the tailgate. They shoved it in and lowered the truck's bed cover.

Denny jumped into the Impala where the keys were still in the ignition. He pulled the Impala around and drove it up on the car trailer.

Meanwhile, Collins walked over to the bloodstains in the ditch and dug up the dead brown grass and dirt with the shovel and turned it all over. Once he had covered the whole area, he patted down the dirt with the back of the shovel to harden it. No blood was showing. He walked to where the back of the car was parked and repeated the procedure where he saw any blood.

He slid the shovel into the bed and closed the tailgate.

Denny got out of the car, strapped its tires down, and drove away. He headed to a favorite cove about three miles into the state forest with an old wagon road and a long ditch. They had buried several bodies there in the past, and no people or animals had ever found them.

The boys had handled the disposal of the body, the car, and had done a complete search of both. Later that night, they broke into the storage unit through a neighboring unit, climbed over the top ceiling, and descended into B322. They searched around until they found the old stove. It was in the back and surrounded by other furniture. They opened it up and found it full of cocaine. Over twenty kilos worth. They looked next to it and found the dryer and washer full as well.

"What the hell are we going to do with that much cocaine?" asked the mayor.

Collins and Denny looked at each other.

Collins had called the mayor from a donut shop parking lot about thirty minutes later. They had scheduled a late-night garage meeting where Collins and Denny had verified all the information.

"Sell it to some gang?" Denny questioned.

The mayor went to work deciding the options and the best possible scenarios to profit. Taking the drugs was the last resort.

"It would take forever to find buyers for that much cocaine," said the mayor. "Too much risk. The best option is to go after the money."

Collins nodded.

"You both will observe the buy, watch for the transfer, follow the money, and hit it on the way home."

Collins knew several places on the routes home that would be perfect. They would approach them in an unmarked car, pull them over, and take them out. They would take the cash and get rid of the bodies. The other gang members might even assume it was stolen or their own guys ran off with it. He crafted a good plan, and all they had to do was follow it.

They all knew there would be a large cash payment being exchanged. They knew when and where it would be, and the anticipated route it would travel. They thought they knew everything. Well, almost everything.

If any of them had thought of this possibility, they would have jumped them much sooner, taking out both rivals. However, it's so much easier in your own backyard to get things accomplished. The mayor had two cops and a judge on his payroll. This kind of protection made any operation outside of Springdale much riskier.

Chapter 5

Mayor King was extremely interested in the night's activities. He was awaiting word that he was going to be two million dollars richer.

The Mayor of Springdale was a fifty-two-year-old former real estate success story named James King. King was a man who showed off his success and wealth. His outward image said look at me. His car collection. His suit collection. His sunglasses and his watches. All were the most extravagant and flashy he could find.

Ego and pride made King an unruly boss and hard to work for. Since he loved showing off, it was tough to keep assistants and employees in general.

King would walk into City Hall, wearing an expensive handmade suit, and begin berating his assistant for his being late to a meeting. His assistants learned to ignore his chest beating and overly dramatic behavior. Little did the average voter know the reality of this man. On TV, a calm and smooth-talking politician emerged. In the privacy of his City Hall, the angry man emerged.

To the public, Mayor King was a self-made man, an example of how to succeed in this world, and especially that wealth is attainable. To them, the mayor had made his money in the real estate market. Everyone knew that.

Twenty years ago, he was a real estate broker in a small town, but with big dreams. All this coming from his stump speech that he gave every four years. Then the housing boom came, and he turned his little office into a large office and hired ten agents and made millions. Local boy becomes a great success.

He had received a call from Collins in the early morning hours, and he was anxious to know the details. None of which were spoken aloud on the phone, or would ever be spoken on a phone. His men were smarter than that. He had reviewed all the ways groups got caught with his men so they would be careful in dealing with him. This call to him had said, "Let's meet." He knew that meant in his detached garage with his collectible cars, a man cave, and a small kitchen. He threw on a pair of jeans, a tee shirt, and a robe and headed out to the garage.

Inside he found the two Springdale Police officers were waiting for him.

"Why are you two here?" said Mayor King.

"We have a problem," said Officer Collins.

"What's the problem?" said the mayor. "Did you forget the plan? You wait till they get on our jurisdiction. You pull them over, kill them, and take the money. Not that hard to understand."

"We didn't need to kill them," said Officer Collins. "The Russians followed them after the deal. I guess they wanted the money and the drugs and had no fear of taking both."

"Where were you two when this was happening?" asked Mayor King.

"We followed them from the casino parking garage," said Officer Denny. "We watched the exchange and saw them hand over five garbage bags in exchange for two duffel bags."

"Two duffel bags," said the mayor. "How much is in them?"

"More than we have ever seen," said Collins.

"Were they full?" asked the mayor.

"Packed, and they looked heavy."

"What happened after that?" asked the mayor.

"We were following the money, just like you told us to. It was a slow drive over the mountains, and it took almost two hours," said Collins. "There was a trailing car that disappeared when we cleared the mountains, and that was when the Russians made their move."

"The Russians were following them after the exchange?" asked the mayor.

"Yes, sir," said Collins. "We didn't notice them until they made their move."

"I think they used a tracker, because they were not in our eyesight the entire time," said Denny. "We were looking for anything."

"Then they came up fast and tried to run them off the road," said Collins. "Gunfire was exchanged, and the chase began. We hung back and followed as best we could. They were headed for our own backyard, so we knew where they would go. They got off the highway and headed down the backroads to the north of County Line Road and Windy Hill. When they got on Windy Hill, we lost them for a minute. They were shooting and one car spun out when it caught a tire in the ditch. The TSG truck took off and made their way to the lake turnout before they lost a tire, either from gunfire or excessive driving. The truck ran off the road and the Russians caught up."

"They shot the hell out of each other," said Denny. "There was only one TSG street thug left alive when we got there, and he was shot in the gut and bleeding out."

"We walked to the back of the truck, but it was empty," said Collins. "We looked all around but we couldn't find anything. They must have ditched it, or someone got away with the bags."

"Could there have been a dead drop or a transfer point along the way?" asked the mayor.

"No, we didn't see anything like that," said Denny.

"You kept eyes on them the whole way?" asked the mayor. "You didn't stop anywhere or fall back too far to see?"

"No."

"Then they probably ditched the money and planned to come back for it," said the mayor.

"Why would they ditch the cash?" asked Denny. "They were trying to protect the cash and get it home."

"Better to take the risk of ditching it than your rivals getting their hands on it," said Collins.

"Well, there is nobody left to get it," said Collins.

"Get back out there and start looking. Stay out there till you find something. If you don't find anything, start canvassing at daybreak," said the mayor. "See if anyone on the route you took saw anything. You two must be the first on the scene. No excuses and take any measures necessary to get the money back."

"If someone opens the bags?" asked Collins.

"Handle it," said the mayor. "You're the police, make up an excuse or law. Tell them it's counterfeit and during a chase it was thrown away. Anything!"

"Yes, Boss," said Collins. "We're on it. Let's roll."

The mayor was nervous and pissed. This was a big score.

Now he had to figure out a plan to find the money and get rid of anybody who knew about it. The money was real. Too many people were dead over those two black duffel bags.

He pushed the button on the garage door.

The door was closing, and he walked under it. He headed back into the house and softly closed the side door. Reaching into his back pocket, he grabbed his gun, placing it in the small upper kitchen cabinet along with his keys.

It was 4:30 in the morning, and there was no way he was going back to bed. He flipped on the kitchen light switch and walked over to the coffee pot. After opening a new bag of arabica beans and grinding them into a perfect drip size, he placed them into a cone shaped filter and set it into the coffee maker. He filled the coffee pot with water, poured it into the water well, flipped the on switch, and waited. This waiting was incredibly good for his mind. He needed quiet. He needed to focus. The solitude of the early morning hours cleared his mind, and he developed a theory.

Mayor King took his coffee into the bathroom and started a shower. When he came out carrying his coffee, he walked into his massively oversized walk-in closet.

Expensive suits lined the walls. The racks were stacked two high, and the clothes wrapped around the room. In the center was a large dresser with drawers on both sides and a marble top.

He walked around the room looking for the perfect suit for this cool morning. He passed suits from some of the finest tailors in the country, as well as from the finest tailors on Savile Row in London. He loved the style, the cut, and the precision involved in quality tex- tiles. When he had decided on a custom-made gray wool suit from a New York tailor, he set his empty coffee cup on the marble.

As he dressed, he kept coming back to the same conclusion: the bags were dropped. He had only two men to find them, and the sun was coming up. Someone was going to find those bags soon, and his guys had to be the first.

He was going to head out and look for the bags himself. He finished dressing, grabbed his cell phone, keys, his gun, and his wallet out of the kitchen cabinet, and headed to his truck. His destination was Windy Hill Road.

The mayor pulled out of his country driveway and headed toward Springdale. He passed through the countryside in the early morning with the window down and the smells of trees and mist heavy in the air. He made it into town and the major four-way intersection with City Hall on one side and the courthouse on the other. The light turned green, and he headed north and out of town toward the connecting road to Windy Hill Road.

Springdale was a town of ten thousand plus, but the census was still several years away. Most estimates put the real population closer to fourteen thousand. Large enough to have a fifteen-officer police force, a city fire department, and all the essential city services. However, it was still small enough to run into church members in the grocery store or see friends and family members walking through the town.

This was a suburban town. It had been a very quaint little town of two thousand about twenty years ago, but thanks to the housing boom, developers had moved in. They built large neighborhoods on cheap farmland. Now the roads had been expanded, shopping centers built, and schools planned and constructed. This was a boom town, and one of the fastest growing areas in the state.

As the Mayor of Springdale, King could manage the economic development of the city to coincide with his own personal agenda.

He was a master at finding a way to shave off a couple points for himself in any deal. No one in town was shrewder, and he made sure that every deal came with confidentiality agreements. These legal documents, which were the size of short novels, helped to distance himself from any wrongdoing and allowed the developer to be personally liable for any information leaked. Since Mayor King had the local judge in his pocket, he was the wrong guy to mess with.

No one talked. Why should they? They were all making tremendous amounts of money. They had their pick of the best properties. The large and vast holdings of the city were available for purchase with the help of the mayor. The mayor's fees were reasonable and never hurt any developers. It was just the cost of doing business. In the end, a mixed-use development could net the developer well over a million dollars. In doing so it created hundreds of new jobs for the community and increased the tax rolls. Who would turn that down?

The city also convinced developers to build parks, playgrounds, and walking trails. The community was happy with everyone because their community was now the envy of the state. They had fine dining restaurants, bars and pubs, new industry, a small lake, and outdoor activities. With the mountains only a few miles away, the quality of life was off the chart. They were starting to be recognized as a great place to live. In addition, they were close to a major city for shopping and excursions but with the benefit of living in a small town. This was a place to be proud of. This was a place to raise a family. This was Springdale.

He had his own little crew of dirty cops and politicians, bankers, and lawyers.

Now was his chance to get bigger, to be a force in the area and eventually take power in the state.

He was an opportunist, and he took big risks. This was the biggest risk he would take. Soon he would learn just how big.

Chapter 6

Early on Saturday morning, two police units started canvassing the area on each end of Windy Hill Road.

Cal had only recently returned from hiding the cash and had managed to lay down on the couch. He was tossing and turning, so he decided to head for his bed. He stood up and stretched while looking at the clock.

As he walked past the window, he saw a vehicle coming down the road at a very slow-moving pace. It had a spotlight. The driver was shining it in the yards and ditches of his neighbors' properties along his road. He quickly closed the curtains and returned to the side of the window to wait. As they approached, he observed the vehicle in the middle of a meticulous search. There were no other cars on the road at 2:30 in the morning, so they had time to search everywhere.

On the right side of the vehicle, which was coming close enough to be identified as a police car, were deep woods. On the left side, a drainage ditch lined the road with the occasional driveway. Occasionally, a small road or driveway would poke out of the woods on the right, but the car was searching everywhere and making sure nothing was left unchecked.

Cal loved his little house and the acreage. It was close to a grocery store, but far enough away to achieve peace and quiet. The only downside was the road in front of his property. It had steadily, over the last several years, become busier and busier. As each new housing development disturbed the natural setting, the road traffic increased. Not only did it destroy the peace and serenity of the local farms, its packed houses were so close together that you could spy on your neighbors from your own kitchen window. The whole thing was reminiscent of a castle courtyard and its gates. Pack all the people into a tight space, surround it with walls, and the populace will feel safe.

Cal did not like the developments, gated communities, or the large cheap houses being quickly assembled on the old farmlands. He felt it was odd to live like sardines packed in a can when the options around him were larger lots with views of the mountains, trees, and hayfields.

The landscaping had taken a long time to clean up and clear out. The growth which had taken over the yard was due to an intricate and well-intentioned gardener. The old couple who'd lived in the home had spent thousands of hours around the house planting and building flower beds. As age made working outside more difficult, the yard and all the many plant varieties grew out of control. The upkeep was too difficult, so everything planted grew wild and became prolific. Later they would move into a local assisted living facility, and the property would be sold by their children.

Now his home, painted inside and out in soothing modern colors and consisting of a large garden; thirty-year-old roses, grapes, apple trees, and azalea bushes; it was a respite in Cal's daily life.

They were slowly checking all the houses and properties along the road. Soon they would reach his pine tree grove.

Cal was watching the approaching car as it was climbing the hilltop. The hayfields were on their left flowing down into the valley below. This hilltop was where most people had placed their houses decades before, seeking to obtain the magnificent view of the sloping valley and a mountain range rising in the distance.

The all-brick rancher about 500 yards to his right was the closest house to him, and the cops were slowing their cruiser and shining their light through the yard, the ditch, and the trees in the forest on their right-hand side.

His place was next and then they would have another mile and a half before the road ended. He had made the right decision, and he felt that now.

He was scared. Scared of losing the money. He could feel his body waking up and getting anxious. Getting those bags to a safe place at that moment was the right call. Why would these cops turn in the money? He certainly would not, so why should they?

How did they know about the money? He saw no police cruisers in the chase. How did they know the bags were dropped? He saw several cars follow the shoot-out, but none of them were police cars. Did they use unmarked cars? Were the cops robbing the criminals? He guessed only time would tell, but for right now, he felt deeply relieved that there was no evidence on his land or in his house of any money.

"Oh crap," he exclaimed. He had forgotten about the money he had grabbed.

He walked down his dark hall into his bathroom where on top of the clothes dryer stood six stacks of $10,000. He took it last night, well, because it was hard not to walk away without something. After lugging all that money across the fields, he deserved something. What good is having money if you can't access it? He also wanted to test it. He had to make sure it was real and legitimate.

He had a plan last night to take it to several different businesses and use it. Let them check it out. Staring at it last night, it appeared real, but what if it was counterfeit? If it was real, he could spend it slowly and no one would be the wiser.

The cops were outside and approaching his house now. However, they did not appear to be stopping at any houses as they were slowly searching for what Cal could only imagine were the bags of money.

He was in good shape. He had time, but he needed to hide the sixty thousand dollars somewhere. He knew that door knocking would be the last resort of the police, but it might happen.

He walked to the window and stared at the police cruiser as it slowly passed his property and the pine grove. The police officers obviously knew how far a bag full of money could be thrown, and they stayed in that search area, but they searched in a meticulous grid pattern for it. Both had spotlights, one on each side of the car. Each light was moving around very rapidly but was missing nothing. Their car was just easing along at maybe five to ten miles an hour. Occasionally, it would slow to a crawl to get a good look at a large rock or bush, and then it would move on. The trees, garbage cans, cars, or anything large would cause a slowdown and a double-check. Most of the houses were set back off the road, so most of the lights were just shining near the edge of the road, the ditch, and the first part of the lawn.

In his hands were stacks of cash. He needed to hide his sixty thousand somewhere good. Besides, they were looking for two giant bags of money and not a couple small stacks. He grabbed all the money and walked to the kitchen. Cal dumped the stacks on the counter and made sure nothing fell on the floor. It was dark, and Cal was being careful as he opened the bright white modern cabinets underneath the kitchen sink and felt around for garbage bags. He found the box and pulled several out. He shook the first one open and continued shaking until it opened all the way. Inside, he placed the six stacks of money but carefully slid one bill out of each stack. He then folded it over many times, pressing all the air out of the bag.

He walked over to the black trashcan with the chrome lid. He grabbed the existing bag in the trashcan with the old Thai food at the top and lifted it out. He then placed the folded black bag with the money in it at the bottom of the trashcan. Then carefully he replaced the trash bag full of ripe-smelling old takeout back into the trashcan and pulled the edges down over the sides, locking it in place.

He folded the six single bills over and placed them next to his wallet on the counter and walked back to the window. He could just see the spotlight in the distance. It was past his house and that was a relief.

He left the receipt on the counter for the Thai food stating it was ten o'clock when he picked it up. He turned on the lights and started cleaning the kitchen.

He thought, I'm a millionaire now, why am I doing my own dishes? He started laughing. "Not yet." Now is not the time to get greedy, he thought. I need to prepare my mind.

Cal finished his dishes, put them in the drying rack. He wiped down the counters with some paper towels and got rid of all the remnants of his takeout food from the previous night.

Saturday morning came quickly, and soon the sun would start to rise over the mountains to the east. The first colors of brownish orange and pink would announce the day. Then a nice orange, red, and slightly yellow tint would appear on this cloudless morning.

Cal sat on his bed trying to force himself back to sleep, but his mind was busy spending money and buying things he could not afford. He was awake. The thought of a fresh cup of coffee was enough for him to give up on the idea of sleeping anyway.

He walked to the refrigerator and took out the eggs and bacon and set them on the counter. He filled the coffee maker with water and ground some beans and waited next to the machine like a kid waiting for Christmas morning to arrive. Cal loved his coffee and made any excuse to make his special-order beans. He looked forward to breakfast simply for the coffee. He wanted a nice strong cup of direct source Costa Rican.

The coffee seemed to take forever. He was tired and had not slept much. Getting up early wasn't his thing, and he could not change his nature. Hopefully, the coffee would do its job soon.

He realized he was hungry and headed back to make eggs, scrambled just like when he was a kid. Cal always believed, in cooking and in life, the old ways were the best ways. He reached into the pantry and grabbed a bottle of water from the twenty-four pack he kept there. He chugged it in one gulp and reached down to grab another. Walking over to the stove, he stretched out his back. His stiffness made him recall the hike and the weight on his back. The pain in his lower back was throbbing and he needed to stretch.

Finally, the coffee maker finished its chore, and Cal poured a fresh cup. He finished it with his usual accoutrements, couple drops of milk and sugar. Then he went to the table to look out at his view.

He pulled out a wooden chair from the table and faced the windows. He slowly sipped his hot coffee while his journey to clear-headed reality continued.

Cal reached down to pet Daisy's head, who was sitting on his feet under the dining room table. As he softly stroked her white fur, he gazed out his windows that looked out onto the hayfields and then to the mountains beyond. His money was out there. Safe for now. The idea that so much money was just sitting in the old barn made him smile. What luck.

His dining room was facing due east. It had been called "very feng shui," at least that was what his realtor had said to him when she showed him the house. It was a word you'd hear but didn't thoroughly understand. The context implied a good location or it produced good vibes. However, he didn't really know what it meant. So many words or concepts we let graze by us daily without taking the time to investigate. It stuck with him, so Cal had Googled it later.

He had learned that feng shui is an ancient science that was developed over 3,000 years ago in China. In a literal translation, feng means wind and shui means water. To the Chinese culture, wind and water were associated with good health, so good feng shui came to mean good fortune. Alternatively, bad feng shui meant bad luck or misfortune.

Feng shui is the art of location and understanding how the placement of yourself and objects within a space affects your life in various ways. Since his house and his windows pointed east to the sunrise, it would somehow balance and harmonize with the energies in his home.

Maybe it was due to the feng shui that bags of money landed in his yard. All that energy was finally being put to good use. The bags were due east of him right now. That thought made him laugh to himself.

He had a strong desire to fully avoid any trouble, so he wanted to get out of the house as fast as he could. At this point, being home was, in his mind, the same as being guilty. Time to get out of the house and avoid any awkward conversations this morning. Those cops out there searching for the bags made him nervous, and he did not want to become a suspect. In about twenty minutes, the road would be busier, and his neighbors would be more active. It was Saturday morning, and this suburban playground was full of house-wives and husbands who would be heading out for the day to shop, get ready for football games, or a plethora of other mind-numbing things to do.

Cal walked over to the window and saw two cars coming down the road. Cal wanted to be joining them real soon. Shopping sound-ed like a good idea. He would take Daisy out for some exercise by the lake, and then on to some Saturday morning shopping.

He needed to test this money, and quickly. If it wasn't real, he would turn it in, and if it was real, no one would ever know.

The big question was where to test it. To him, the bills looked very authentic. However, he needed to hand it to somebody who saw a lot of cash. Cal didn't carry cash anymore. It was rare that he ever used it. Being on the road, every expense went through his American Express card, for the points. Everything was about the points. He liked earning his credit card points, hotel points, and airline miles, and he was good at it. He did not even have a traditional wallet to carry cash, as he used a small front pocket wallet.

He gathered his things, his keys, the leash, and his wallet. He whistled for Daisy, and she came running to the door. He always felt so bad for leaving Daisy locked up in the house or kennel during the week. He was gone for eight to ten hours at a time, and he felt that on the weekends she should get to go with him most places.

Cal and Daisy exited through the side door and into the garage. He pushed the garage door button, and it started to slowly open. Daisy did not wait, she never did, and darted under the door off to her favorite spot to handle her business, which in this case was sniffing and circling around the area where she finally squatted to pee.

He walked over to the car, leaned on it, and watched as Daisy did her thing. He could hear cars coming down the road more frequently now, and he felt safe heading out. He whistled for Daisy, and she came running as he opened the door to the back seat of his white Jeep Cherokee, and she jumped inside.

Cal pushed the start button and waited for a moment as the heater warmed up. He pulled up the hill and onto the main road heading right out of his driveway and away from town. The light was brighter now with only a few shadows on the road from the dark tree canopy.

Daisy sat up on her hind end in the back seat staring out the front window. She loved riding in the car, being with Cal, and of course sticking her head out of the window, but it was too chilly for that. Cal had the heater on and had no interest in cooling the car off. They rode together in silence for about three miles, Cal being hyperaware of every car passing and keeping his eye out for any more bags along the side of the road or evidence of the chase that occurred just nine plus hours ago. He saw no police officers, bags, or anything out of the ordinary.

Cal made sure he was not speeding. The speed limit was forty-five miles an hour, and he was driving smoothly around the twists and turns of this country road heading towards a wider road near the lake.

He drove up to and turned into the Springdale Lake Recreation area. This area had large houses on the perimeter and had been established to save a small piece of the lake for the public. This was a boater's lake, and already this morning he could see three or four fishing boats making their way around the edges and bridges. Lake Desoto was not the largest of lakes. In fact, it was a dammed-up river, but it had great fishing, boating, and several marinas.

Cal decided to go to the hilltop where there was a great view overlooking the lake. He wanted a great place to think, and lack of sleep was slowing him down. He continued his drive up the small grass-lined road toward a picnic area overlooking the water, parking near the edge of a picnic table and barbecue pit. Climbing out of the car, he put his gloves on and then let Daisy out of the back seat to run around. Being cold outside, this place would be vacant still for many months, which made it a great place to throw the Frisbee with your dog, find some peace of mind, or give you time to think. Daisy wanted the playtime and Cal needed to think.

Cal climbed up on top of the picnic table with a view of the water below. The water was made up of two distinct colors. Closer to him, the water was gray blue and very calm with only a small shimmer on the surface. Out in the main channel, the water turned darker gray and appeared to move more dramatically. The fish would be biting this morning, and the weather was perfect.

He felt confident in his hiding place, and he was sure no one would ever find his stash of cash. It was almost a half mile from the road, and the whole area was overgrown and not traveled. So he relaxed a little bit. After all, he was rich.

An older woman in a blue and white jogging outfit approached him. She was walking a small white dog with a puffy coat.

"Good morning," she said.

Cal looked up and gave the reply, "Morning."

"Can my Isabel say hello to your dog?"

"Sure, come here, Daisy."

Daisy came running and said hello to the dog.

"Did you hear about the marina?" the woman asked.

"No," replied Cal. "What happened?"

"A shootout here in Springdale, can you believe it?"

"No, I can't."

"Apparently it's gang related. They killed themselves. Each side shooting the other."

"Really? Unbelievable."

"You have a great day," she said. "Come on, Isabel."

"Daisy, sit."

As the old lady was walking away, he asked himself, "They are all dead?"

The money has to be his now. How lucky it was, but how terrible that everyone died. What was he going to do?

Wait, he thought. A gang is not a couple of people. Now he knew it was gang money. This was not great news, but he knew that amount of money was most likely for illegal activities.

Would the gangs come to his house and expect to find the bags where their comrades had left it?

This was not good. It meant that he was missing things and he needed to stay sharp. To safely get out of this situation with the money, he needed to set some guidelines or rules to live by.

Cal laid back on the table, eyes to the sky, and thought to himself, what do I need to be doing or not doing?

Rule #1 - don't spend the money in public. This is how criminals and tax cheats always got caught. You see it in the movies; a guy pulls off a bank heist but gets caught driving a new Corvette with no job. No red flags. Find a way to move and invest the money, but still have access to it.

Rule #2 - don't go back to the money until it is safe to do so. The worst thing to do is lead others to the hiding place.

Rule #3 - no unusual behavior. Don't leave for two months. "I must keep up appearances." Go to work, go home, rinse and repeat.

He drifted off to sleep for a little while, and eventually, Daisy came over and nuzzled his face. She was done sniffing around and wanted to play.

He felt better. He sat up on the table, regaining his composure and repeating the rules to himself as he sat there.

Time to move around. Plus, he could not think of any more rules. The sun was now shining down on the lake and creating a strong reflection.

He stood up grabbed the Frisbee off the table and heaved it into the grass field. Daisy took off after it, her white fur raising and lowering as she ran. She missed the jump and the Frisbee bounced and started rolling in a half circle. She ran up to it and bit down hard. Picking it up with a crunch, she ran back to Cal. He walked over and opened the driver's side door. Pulled his sunglasses out of the visor holder and walked over to Daisy who was waiting for the next dozen throws. He obliged her and before long she flopped down on the ground in front of him, exhausted and panting.

Cal sat down in the cool grass with his legs extended, and Daisy laid her head across his knees. This was a great day. He felt great and carefree. For the moment, he was rich and safe.

Twenty minutes later, he was driving to the grocery store to try out his newfound wealth. Daisy was asleep in the back seat; the panting had stopped. He drove around the winding roads for five and half miles until he pulled into the parking lot of the grocery store. Progress was great. He lived in the country, but he had a grocery store just down the road now. Bonus, they had just built a new Starbucks in front of it. These were the types of places that dealt in cash. This would be a good place for a test, that money marker thing or the new scanner they had. Either one would give him the answer he needed. If it was counterfeit, the store would confiscate it, and he would say that he got it in exchange somewhere. No big deal.

As he approached the grocery store, he saw there were only a few cars in the parking lot, so he headed on past the large parking lot, the tax preparer, the bank, and the pizza place. He pulled off at the Starbucks entrance and made his way into the line that was already six cars deep. He was contemplating if he should go through the drive-through or go inside. In the end, he just didn't want to leave Daisy in the car, so he went into the drive-through line and inched along until he got to the ordering board. "Hope you're having a wonderful day so far, what can I get started for you?" said the overly happy voice coming over the speaker.

"Grande Americano with two sugars and 2% milk."

"$3.44," said the voice, and he pulled forward.

He reached the window and pulled a hundred dollar bill out of his right jean pocket and handed it to the young woman with dark black hair, bright red lipstick, and a nose ring.

"Do you have anything smaller; I don't think I can break this?" she asked.

"No, sorry."

"Let me check with my manager."

She took it into the store and the window closed behind her. Cal waited, tapping his fingers on the steering wheel and trying to remain calm.

A few moments later, she came back holding his change in one hand and his Americano in the other, passing both through the window. He thanked her and dropped the cash on the seat next to him, placing the drink into his cup holder. He told her thank you again and pulled out of the line and into the grocery store parking lot.

"It worked!" he exclaimed.

That was a great first step. It had to be real. One more test to do. One for two is not bad, let's see what happens here. He cracked all the windows, told Daisy he would be right back, and went in to buy some hot dogs and beer.

As he walked through the automatic doors, a gust of heat hit him hard in the face, reminding him he had been outside for a while. He walked through the checkout line and headed to the back of the store. On the way, he stopped by the bread aisle and grabbed hot dog buns. He then went to the refrigerated section and grabbed some hot dogs. Then a trip to the beer aisle to grab a six-pack of Heineken and he was done. He headed toward the front. As he passed the endcap of the aisle, he noticed a large gift card stand with every kind of gift card imaginable. He had an idea. He grabbed a gift card with a fifty-dollar value and walked to the cashier.

He placed all his items on the moving checkout counter and watched as the young girl with the striped grocery store shirt swiped all the items.

"How are you today?" she said smiling. "Did you find every-thing you needed?"

"Doing good," Cal said. "All good."

"Your total is $72.45," she said.

Cal reached into his pocket, produced a $100 bill, and handed it over. She grabbed a black marker and swiped it on the bill. She then stuffed it under the drawer in the cash register and made change, handing him his cash, his bag, and a big smile.

"Have a nice day!"

Cal left the store grinning from ear to ear.

Chapter 7

Luis was on his phone. He was sending texts to several of his contacts. His goal was to get in contact with someone who could reach out and act as a middleman to open communications again with the Russians. His original Russian contacts were not answering him. He was now almost positive they had tried to double-cross him. Take the money and the drugs, have it all.

Luis had thought out this same conclusion. He had run every scenario and concluded he would lose half his crew in a bad decision like this. Now he had been pulled into it. He was determined to play this right. He needed a plan. He thought of Crazy Eddie, and how he got here twenty years ago. He needed to deal with the Russians in the same way.

Luis was a lifer; he had joined the gang when he was twelve. His first job was hustling out a living on a corner. He was selling small crack bags for ten dollars.

The gang often used kids as an intermediary for criminal activity. They were often left alone by cops, rivals, and customers.

He was a smart kid, and no one ever got one over on him. He took care of his business and never missed a payment. Soon, he was moving up in the gang. He hit his first rival gang member when his corner was absorbed by an enterprising rival gangster when he was only thirteen.

Rooftop put his phone down on the desk and leaned back in his chair. For some reason, the Crazy Eddie events were coming back to him, and he was having trouble thinking of anything else. He knew why, but he decided to rehash the whole thing in his mind all over again.

Luis' corner was on the borderland of the two rival gangs. The Thirteenth Street Gang, or TSG, controlled a large area, more than forty streets, but the rival Black Titans Gang wanted that corner.

An ambitious dealer wanting to expand his business saw the young dealer on the corner as an easy mark. He and three of his members decided to rob young Luis at night. They drove up and pretended to buy. When he produced the smack, they pulled their guns. They took all the cash on him and his supply.

Luis figured one day this would happen. The gang's protection was a deterrent to most white- and blue-collar buyers, but not to rival gangs.

He had hiding holes in alleyways and under buildings all over his street. He hid his supply in three different places, his money in two places, and a gun under the loading dock of an abandoned factory.

He figured he would never need the gun except for revenge, but that time was now. He lost about a hundred dollars and ten bags of smack. All in all, about two hundred dollars. A totally acceptable loss to the gang. Cops shook down the gang members for a lot more all the time.

To Luis, it was the message it sent. His corner was not theirs, and he would not be running back to the gang to get reassigned, or to get help.

This was his turf and he was going to defend it.

He came up with a plan. He went dark for a week and could not be found anywhere. His one appearance at the gang HQ was to make his cash drop. He had never missed a payment, and he never would.

Luis was living on the rooftop of an abandoned building diagonal to his corner. From this vantage point he observed the new dealer, Crazy Eddie. That was the name he had heard from down below. Several times Crazy Eddie was alone on the corner, and several times he had some kids working the corner.

Luis was going to get his corner back, but he was going to do it the right way.

Luis collected several things over the next couple days. He stole a car from the Black Titan's neighborhood. A beat-up old Dodge Dart, brown and rusted and probably wouldn't be missed. He stole it from the garage of an old lady's house. It was immaculate inside, and in the glove box was a copy of the registration for every year going back to 1972. No money. The only other items in the car were clip-on sunglasses to go over top of prescription glasses.

Luis also gathered some weapons. He had never felt unsafe before, so he had not had a need for weapons. He bought a knife; a five-inch folding blade knife with a wood handle. He also got his gun and five bullets from its hiding place. The rusty old snub nose thirty-eight was in bad shape. He spent two nights oiling and cleaning it until it was a presentable weapon and he was sure it would not blow his hand off when fired.

After four days of observing the corner. Luis saw four different dealers working there. Crazy Eddie only came by at night to collect the money now. He had set up four dealers to handle the day-to-day. Business had fallen off dramatically at first, as the tides changed. Now it was back to normal. This was his money and his corner. He felt as if his inheritance had been stolen from him. This was the first time since his mother died he felt like he belonged somewhere and he owned something. He would rather die than give it up.

That night, he went to work.

The first dealer was the hardest. He was eighteen, black, and strong. Luis walked up to him and, taking no chances, slashed his throat when the dealer reached into his pocket for a dime bag. The boy would not die easily. He reached around and grabbed a gun from his back pocket and the struggle began. It spilled into the side alley and out of sight, but by the end of it, the boy was dead and Luis was covered in his blood.

Luis pilfered through his pockets and took everything. A nice haul. $340 in cash, twenty bags of smack, and a gun with a handful of bullets.

He dragged the boy around the side of the building where he had a hand truck waiting. He tied his lifeless body to the hand truck and wheeled his victim to the abandoned auto shop and the waiting trunk of the Dart.

He went back to his place, washed up, and changed clothes. He hid his money and drugs in various stash spaces.

Then he went back to the vantage point on top of the building. From the roof drainage hole, he could see the corner below illuminated in streetlight.

He waited for an hour. Crazy Eddie was late tonight.

Eventually, Crazy Eddie showed up looking for his cash. He looked around, waited for ten minutes, and then took off in a huff.

Luis was laughing to himself on top of the building.

"Gotcha," he whispered.

The next day was a cash drop day, and Luis made his on time.

Luis was just thirteen years old and was officially initiated into the Thirteenth Street Gang. He would make every drop and do everything asked of him. He had respect, a family, and support when he needed it. He would not give it up.

He stayed at HQ when the associated member who he pushed up to invited him to stay for a barbeque.

Luis ate until he was hardly able to move. All the members did. These types of events were invite only, and Luis was honored to be there.

The liaison officer, a full member and a lower boss of the organization, came over and started talking to Luis. Luis did not know his name, but he went by Bullseye. Bullseye wanted to know if he had been bothered by the neighboring Titans.

Luis told him he had been harassed and even mugged once, but he was handling it.

"You still made your drop?"

"I did," Luis said.

"How? Your own money?"

"No, sir," he retorted. "I took it back!"

"Respect, but be careful. You still need to report in, just in case. We will have your back, but only if we know to watch it."

"*Entiendo*," Luis said.

"Tell Jimmy he is there to help you. Do you need some extra hands this week? Just to be sure."

"No, sir," Luis blurted. "I'll handle it myself."

"I bet you will, little man. I'll get you a gun."

"I have one," Luis said with a grin.

"You are full of surprises. I've been told that in a year you have never missed a cash drop. That is rare. Everyone gets robbed, shook down, or just come up short in sales. But not you. You never miss. Why?"

"I just keep going. If something happens, I fix it," Luis stated. "If sales are slow, I move or work longer hours. I am serious about membership."

"You sure are. I have plans for you, kid. Keep it up!"

"If you need something, come to me. *Adios, amigo*."

Luis left the largest lunch of his life and made his way back to his rooftop storage room. He could live with the other initiates in the bunkhouses, but he was not interested. He wanted his privacy and to be on his own. Besides, several of those kids had already been busted, shot, or even killed. Hair-brained ideas and big scores were common storylines when he was around those boys. Their way into the membership was not hard work or steady success. Meanwhile, they spent every penny they made on cigarettes, drugs, or booze. They were even in debt to other members. Their focus was always a big score. They needed it to break free.

Luis worked differently.

He went over to his mattress and flopped down and took a nap. Three hours later, he woke up to the sounds of honking horns. He slowly walked over to the edge, got down on all fours, and looked out the drainage hole. He saw Eddie and three men. They were looking for the missing boy. Cursing and horn honking followed.

"Where is that little…" Eddie was shouting. "Missed his drop… better not be shooting up."

Luis was smiling. He loved to see the disorder.

It was early evening and Eddie put one of his guys on the corner with a tall bag. He wanted to make up for last night.

Luis was ready for this. He went back to bed.

Later that night, Luis took the back fire escape down to the street and worked his way around the building. It was dark with the only light on the corner coming from the streetlight. Luis walked slowly around, looking up and down both streets. Seeing no one, he walked up to his old sitting position under the old signage and against the front doors of the building across the street. He sat on the ground about ten feet away from the new dealer.

"Hey!" said the young and tattooed black teenager. "Get lost."

"So tired," said Luis.

The teenager approached Luis and kicked his outstretched feet.

"I said get the hell outta here."

"Nah, man. Too Tired."

The teenager exploded at Luis and grabbed him with both hands, lifting him up. Luis came alive and thrusted a knife deep into the teenager's chest.

Stunned, the teenager dropped Luis to the ground and started to cry out, but Luis prevented this with a quick slash of the throat.

The teenager fell in a pool of blood. With this quick action, Eddie was missing yet another dealer.

The take was two hundred and thirty dollars and sixty-two bags of smack.

Luis was making out well. He usually only pocketed about ten to twenty dollars a night, for a lot of risk, but this was entry-level. Not much for an adult, but for a street kid it was enough to thrive.

Now, Luis had over eighty bags of smack worth over eight hundred dollars of complete profit, and he had plenty of cash.

Fridays were paydays and the busiest day of the week. The sales on those nights could be over five hundred. His take was ten percent. The more he sold, the more he made. The ultimate multi-level marketing. His cash was bumped up to Jimmy Rodriguez, then split again with his officer, and then up the ladder to the top.

One dollar on ten was enough to make most initiates cry. Most would sell fifty to seventy-five bags a week on their corners. More on the weekend. Not Luis. He saw the potential. He pushed almost two hundred. While others were trying to sell a dime bag for twenty to make eleven dollars, Luis would keep his price and push more. He would hit street corners after the other initiates went to bed.

Jimmy brought him food all the time, benefits, plus Jimmy loved having Luis as an initiate. He worked hard and was worth two or three other dealers.

Jimmy had promised to never tell anyone else where Luis lived. So far, he had kept his promise.

Luis respected Jimmy and saw him to move up. If he moved Jimmy up, he could move into Jimmy's role. Teamwork and cunning were already working hard developing a career for Luis.

Three days passed slowly, and Luis made another payment to Jimmy. He hung out on the rooftop for almost all that time. He was watching for Eddie and who he might send to his corner.

The place was completely empty for the first day. Luis assumed Eddie was watching who would come around, hoping it was something simple like a rival fighting over the corner. It was a good corner and had a good repeat business. Luis was missing out on dollars, but he did not care. This was far more interesting. The psychology of a gangster. What would Eddie do next?

Luis lived on bread and peanut butter for the next two days. He was earning his nickname of Rooftop. In fact, he did not come off the roof for a whole week. Jimmy came to see him for his drop. He told him he was sick, and Jimmy came back with some soup and wished him well. Jimmy collected his money, on time again, and left.

Luis was watching, always watching his corner. He had set up three lookout blinds around the roof to get different angles on the streets below.

He saw some of Eddie's men in an SUV the night before, just watching to see what happened.

Tonight, Eddie pulled up in his IROC with the radio blasting. It sat on the corner for about five minutes and then one of the men got out, a tattooed monster of a man. He was in his twenties, at least six foot five, with bulging arms and a puffed-up chest.

He strolled over to the corner and leaned against the building.

Soon a trickle of buyers braved the new guy and his muscles, and the money started rolling in. Eddie must have figured no one would dare mess with this guy.

Luis was in awe. Eddie's reaction was one of strength. A common one. Someone threatens you, puff up and act strong.

Eddie, in his inability to think differently, was pushing ahead. To him, the new territory was the goal. A chance to expand his territory and his income. He would put on a show for a while. Luis would wait him out.

The next morning, Jimmy stopped by with a breakfast burrito and a stack of old books.

"I brought you something," Jimmy said.

"What's that?"

"Knowledge, my young friend."

"Knowledge?"

Jimmy was excited to share. "I see how you are always thinking and planning ahead. I brought you a master in that area. Read this first. It's called *The Art of War* by Sun Tzu."

"What is it about?"

"Strategy," Jimmy smiled. "It's how to win battles before they are even fought."

"Really, I might like that."

"I thought so. I also brought you some great books I have read a few times. Some are from my English classes before I dropped out of school. They are good. You will probably like 'em."

"Thanks, man!" Luis was excited.

Luis did not read much, but he did not have much else to do watching from the rooftop all day.

"No problem, brother," Jimmy replied. "Just get 'em back to me when you're done."

"I will."

"Oh, I almost forgot, here is a new bag of product, fifty bags, and a sausage burrito."

"Let me get you the cash," Luis stated.

"No worries, no need to prepay."

"Naw, I got it," Luis retorted. "No biggie."

Luis went to his cabinet and counted out four hundred and fifty dollars. He walked over and handed it to Jimmy.

Jimmy was not understanding. "You sure?"

"Yeah, save me a trip," Luis said, and then flopped back down on his bed with the burrito in his hand. "Thanks for the burrito. I'm starving."

"Your appetite back?" Jimmy asked.

"Oh yeah." Luis took a large bite and began chewing slowly.

"Good man, well I'll see you at the end of the week."

"OK, thanks."

"Read those books," Jimmy was saying as he closed the door.

Luis would read the books. Money and respect was the most important thing to him. He wanted to earn his place, and he would do anything to achieve his goal. Nothing was off limits to Luis, and he was becoming a giant. He was becoming the most feared gangster around, and anyone who messed with him would end up dead.

Chapter 8

Cal was feeling extraordinary. More than just satisfied. He was rich. Really rich. The money was real.

Now what? Fear was starting to dart into his mind.

Those who threw the bags would no doubt come looking, unless they were all dead. It was risky to assume that conclusion. His mind was trying to justify hiding the money. It was also trying and failing to think this was over. This was way too easy. Money couldn't just fall into your yard and then you got to spend it. No, this would get worse before it got better.

No way would he turn it over. He was not crazy. The rational part of him was sure that whoever he turned it over to would make sure he would disappear. The amount of money was too much for anyone to resist. The situation was too easy for anyone to take advantage of. He was alone and remote. Killing him would be easy and no one else would know about the money.

Any gang member coming back would have that simple thought in his mind. Any corrupt or even slightly corrupt cop would think the same. This was not going to be easy after all.

There was one solution. He could drive to the police station in full view of everyone and dump the bags on the counter. If everyone could see it. He would be safe. However, that would involve giving up the money, which he was no longer prepared to do.

He had friends, family, and coworkers who would probably offer great advice, but that would put more people at risk. No, he had to do this on his own. Cal really wanted to tell someone. Who would not want to tell the world, or at least a good friend? "Hey, you'll never believe what happened to me last night."

He had won the lottery, but bragging could get you killed. He had no one he could share the excitement with. All the feelings of excitement, adrenaline, and fear were building up inside of him. He felt like he would explode.

He remembered Rule #3; play it cool, Cal, and keep it normal. It is Saturday. What do I do on Saturday? It was too cool to mow the lawn. He had already played with Daisy and she was tired. He could go shopping, but Rule #1 was coming back to him. Let's not go spending a bunch of money right now. Maybe a small purchase or two.

Right now, he had to contain his emotions. He would detach from most everyone he knew for a while. He would be normal, but even more boring than usual.

Maybe a movie, but sitting still for two hours made him change his mind. He had to get out of the house; sitting on the couch waiting for something to happen was creating too much anxiety.

He reached down and patted Daisy on the head. "Be back soon, girl," he said. He grabbed his things and went out through the garage. As he was heading toward his car, a Springdale Police cruiser turned into his driveway.

He stood there as stiff as a board. Daisy began barking from the front window. The cruiser pulled into the driveway very slowly, positioning itself behind his Jeep, blocking him in, and making Cal feel even more nervous. The officer in the car had his window down and Cal approached.

"Good morning, Officer," he said.

The officer had dirty blond hair, looked about thirty-five to forty years old, and wore a dark blue uniform with a bulletproof vest that puffed up his chest. This man appeared to be in great shape

His nametag said Denny.

"Is this your house?" said the officer.

"It is, can I help you?"

"We are just asking people on your road if they saw anything suspicious or out of the ordinary last night."

"No, not to my knowledge."

"Were you at home last night?" asked Denny.

"I was, I got in around ten o'clock. I was in Knoxville for work and got back late."

Denny followed up, "Did you see or hear anything suspicious last night?"

"No, not that I remember," replied Cal. "I was exhausted. I tried to watch TV but fell asleep. I went to bed shortly after getting home."

Daisy was at the window still barking. The officer turned and looked at her. "What about this morning, have you seen anything out of the ordinary?"

"No," said Cal shaking his head. "What are you looking for?"

Denny started looking back to the road. "There was a disturbance down the road last night.

Denny opened the car door and shuffled his large body out of the car.

Cal could see his massive figure at about six foot three, but wide as a door.

"I am just doing some follow-ups, checking with the neighbors. Heard from some of your neighbors up the road earlier. They heard gunshots late last night. When we get a report of suspicious activity, we routinely check the area."

"What was going on with the gunshots? Domestic disturbance?"

"No, it appears there was a shootout and robbery of some possible gangbangers down near the marina last night," Denny said while searching around and not looking at Cal.

Cal looked shocked. "Gangbangers around here?"

"No cause for concern, we feel they were just passing through the area and got caught up in an exchange that somehow went south," said Denny. "Honestly, it looks like they ended up killing each other, so that problem really kind of solved itself."

"Passing through?"

"Yeah, some of the gangs in Atlanta and Knoxville tend to do their business deals outside of their normal areas," Denny explained. "Less people who can ID them, and less chance of getting caught."

"You said they were all dead," Cal replied. "At the marina? Who were they?" asked Cal.

"We have not released that information yet."

"Do they know what they were doing here?" asked Cal. "What gangs were they in?"

"Again, no information yet."

Denny started walking up the driveway and began looking in the ditch next to the road. His eyes followed the ditch to the pine grove where Cal had been just last night. The pine trees created a large blanket of pine needles on the ground about two inches thick.

"What are you looking for?" asked Cal. In it, Cal could see the slightly disturbed ground where the heavy bags had hit the ground the night before. He walked around and said, "No guns. What do I do if I find anything?"

Denny was looking around. "Just give us a call," he said. He handed Cal his business card. "Don't open any packages or bags. These guys sometimes lace the bags and zippers with LSD and other nasty things as a safety precaution."

"Really?"

"Oh yes, you could be on the ground, shaking uncontrollably in no time. Call us and we will handle it."

"No problem," said Cal. "You're my first call."

"Sounds good," said Denny. He turned and started walking toward his cruiser. "Have a nice day."

"You too."

Denny wiggled into the car, which was still running, said something on his radio, and slowly backed out of the driveway and onto the road. He waved as he headed down the road and to the next house.

Cal walked back to his garage and back into his house. He was sweating, and his shirt was wet. When did he start sweating? The encounter he was dreading was now over, but he was still sweating and nervous. Could Officer Denny see him sweating? Luckily, he had his North Face jacket over top, so Denny could not see all of it.

He walked back to his bedroom and stripped off his jacket and shirt. He threw the wet shirt in the laundry bin and grabbed a fresh one out of his dresser. He got dressed again and headed back to the dining room.

He needed coffee. He was feeling weak and tired now. The adrenaline was wearing down, and he had accumulated little sleep. Where was the coffee he had bought? The car. He had forgot all about it. He walked outside and opened the car door and got his coffee out of the cup holder. It was slightly cool. He brought it inside and stuck it in the microwave for thirty seconds and warmed it up. After the timer rang, he grabbed the cup, and walked back to his chair. Daisy sat at his feet. He slowly took a sip of coffee, which smelled funny. He looked at the side of the cup, and he could see a burn mark near the bottom. Something in the cup had reacted to the microwave. He got up and poured the coffee in the sink and threw away the cup.

He called Daisy and she came outside with him and got into the back seat of the Jeep. He pulled out of the driveway and headed back to Starbucks. Fortunately, he had plenty of change.

He arrived at Starbucks, got out and cracked the windows, deciding to go inside this time. He repeated his order, got his coffee, and sat down at a corner table to calm himself and enjoy his coffee. He could see Daisy sitting in the driver's seat staring at the main door and the flow of customers.

Cal pulled out his cell phone and started checking his emails and getting caught up. There were two emails from family. One from his mom in Florida where she had retired four years ago after working as an ER nurse for thirty-six years. An email from his sister about his nephew's birthday party which was coming up in a week. A pool party with twenty-five nine-year-olds. Sounds like hell, he thought.

He checked his work email as well. A note from his boss saying his bonus check would be a week late since the last day of the month fell on a Wednesday. Nothing new there. His quarterly bonuses were nice, but nothing to brag about. He hardly noticed them after they were deposited. The bank account swallowed most every check, no matter the size, and at the end of the month, same as before. He stood up and walked back to his car. He sat in the driver's seat and slowly sipped his coffee and was feeling calmer.

His encounter with Officer Denny had scared him. He needed to get control of his anxiety or he was going to be a real mess. Forget about sleeping or eating or anything really. This was going to possess his life.

***

Denny was in the parking lot of the grocery store observing Cal as he went into the Starbucks and got back into his Jeep. Denny had narrowed the search to just five or six houses and a handful of fields where the money could be. The time when the lead cars got out of sight, Cal's house was one of them.

Cal had slightly bloodshot eyes, he seemed a bit nervous, and the pine needles in his yard seemed disturbed next to the road, which was the only area he had seen with that kind of ground disturbance all night. He texted Collins. "We need to meet. Near Starbucks parking."

Collins responded, "Five minutes."

After watching Cal sit in his car for a few minutes, Denny saw Collins pull up next to him in his cruiser with his window down. "What you got?" Collins asked.

Denny turned and looked at him. "The guy over there is Calvin Wilson," Denny said softly. "He owns the small house on Windy

Hill near the hayfields. He was a little off, and the ground near his ditch and the pine trees looked a little disturbed."

"Disturbed, could be critters or just walking on pine needles, you know that."

"I am just informing you of a possible lead."

"What did he say?"

"Nothing, acted oblivious."

"Anything else?"

"He has a dog, but it's in the car with him. Now would be a good time to check his place out."

"I'm on my way."

Collins pulled out of the lot and headed toward Cal's house.

Three minutes later, he was pulling off on an old, abandoned farm road which hid his car from the road, about three hundred yards from Cal's driveway. Collins got out and started walking through the field. He could see the back of Cal's house and started walking toward it.

His car was just hidden, but if anyone was looking, it appeared as if he was running radar. However, the car was empty. This was an opportune time to investigate the outbuilding and the back side of the house. Look underneath if there was a crawl space. The usual outside hiding places for something large.

Collins was walking around the fence line and was only partially visible from the road on his left. The road was higher up and the cars were moving quickly. There was little risk of being seen. He was trying to avoid the soft patches of grass and mud which were the result of tractor wheel tracks and hay balers leaving swaths of torn up ground and muddy tracks behind them. Luckily for him, there were still long streaks of cut brown grass missed by the baler and laying diagonally on the ground. These made a great walking path over the sloppy field. The fall and winter rains had been heavy this year, and the result had been pooling in the fields.

He could wait till dark, but with the dog in the house or yard, this would be much easier. The hard part was to find a perfect way into the property without being seen.

He was almost near the backyard fence. The clouds had moved in, and it appeared as if it might rain at any minute. He moved quickly to the little shed in the backyard. He saw no lock on the door. He pulled it open and drew his flashlight and conducted a thorough search. Inside the little building he found an old lawn mower sitting on the floor and yard tools neatly stacked on the sides. An old bug zapper hung from a hook in the back right corner, but that was it. He checked the floor and saw no loose boards or anything out of the ordinary. He exited the shed and closed it back up.

Moving along the line of the shed, he moved up around the back porch, looking underneath and checking everywhere. The bags he saw being loaded into the truck the previous day were not easy to hide. They were over two feet long. Also, there were two of them. He searched high and low. He even walked quickly up to the front of the house and searched under the front porch and walked to the pine grove. He could see some footprints and some disturbed pine needles, but nothing conclusive. This was probably another dead end, but they needed to check out every possibility.

Most of the old farmers they had spoken to on the road already were hardly able to get to the door. They would not have dared to move heavy bags out of a ditch. Some houses were for sale, and one was missing its owner. He would go there after this to check again because he was finding no trace here.

Just then he got a text. "On the move."

He quickly headed toward the field and left the property.

He drove to the house down the road and saw no activity for the second time today. He walked up to the door and knocked this time. A seven-year-old and his grandma came to the door. Collins began his rehearsed line.

They had heard and seen nothing. The owner of the house was sleeping. She worked the night shift, and the grandma and kid were asleep last night by nine.

As he left the driveway and headed for his cruiser, he grabbed his phone and sent a text to Denny. "Dog's house tonight."

It was their only option.

Chapter 9

The sun was down, and most of Cal's neighbors were inside and getting ready for bed, when Denny and Collins pulled Denny's truck into the abandoned farm road off Windy Hill Road.

Denny looked at his watch and said, "9:45."

He turned off the truck's lights and waited for their eyes to adjust to the darkness.

"Let's watch for a little while," Collins said. "Keep your eye out for any neighbors."

After twenty minutes, the two men exited the truck and started making their way toward the open field. Each wore black pants, sweaters, and black ski masks. Black combat boots completed their ensembles.

Inside the house, the lights were on. They could see movement in the house, and at 10:15 pm they saw the back door open and a light-haired dog rush out. They each dropped to one knee. The dog rushed out quickly to a spot in the yard. It squatted after ten seconds of circling around and around. The dog then rushed back to the door, where Cal was waiting. The door closed.

"Looks like he could be getting ready for bed," whispered Collins.

"Perfect," retorted Denny.

"Let's wait till the lights go out," said Collins.

Denny said, "What do you want to do about the dog?"

"I brought the tasers, quiet and should do the trick," Collins whispered back.

"Let's move in closer," said Denny.

"No, that dog will give us away," said Collins. "We need to get closer and have the element of surprise."

Denny smiled and said, "You always have a plan, what did you have in mind?"

"We are going to split up," said Collins.

***

Cal had just let Daisy out for the night. He walked over and shoved half of the small frozen pizza into the refrigerator. Earlier, he had thought he was starving, but today, all food and drink seemed destined to be wasted. He began turning off the lights while making his way to the bathroom. He brushed his teeth and felt more and more tired as he completed his regular pre-bed routine. His exhaustion was most likely the result of the adrenaline and excitement of the last twenty-four hours finally wearing off.

He had spent the last several hours researching the shootout down the road near the marina and the lake road turnout.

The best reporting on the situation said it was a gang-related shooting. Two rival gangs had converged on the same deal. That was when things went wrong. According to the *Knoxville Sun*, the Thirteenth Street Gang members, or TSG, were meeting for a drug buy when the two parties most likely came to a disagreement, and one of the rival gangs, either TSG or the Russians, started shooting. All the men were armed, and the FBI had seized eleven weapons on the scene. A massive gun fight erupted. Probably quick and deadly. All participants were quickly wounded, with all eventually dying at the scene. Some bled out over a longer period, and some died instantly. The Knoxville Gang Unit had come up to Springdale to process and help make sense of the situation. The ATF and FBI were now also involved. The amount of illegal and unique types of weapons were of interest to all parties. No drugs or money were found at the scene. It was assumed that if there were survivors, they made off with all the spoils. This was the first time anything like this had occurred near Springdale.

The spokesperson for the Knoxville Gang Unit said, "It appears as if our efforts to stop this kind of activity has pushed these transactions out of our territory and into neighboring areas. We will be coordinating activities with Springdale and other neighboring police departments to stop the spread of gang activities and violence."

Cal thought he had a good understanding of what was happening. He had also watched the ten o'clock news; it was the lead story. No new information was discovered, or discussed, but there was an onsite reporter standing next to the police tape and spotlights with crime scene investigators mulling around in the background.

Cal had been at the lake this morning and had seen zero activity. He had gone to the park across the lake, but it was surprising that he had seen nothing at all out of the ordinary.

Cal's mind drifted back to the money and what it represented. His freedom. Of course, it could buy many things, and it could improve his life dramatically. However, what Cal desired more than anything was a change in direction. He was stagnant. He went to work every Monday and did the same tasks throughout the week.

His job had its rewards, and he did like it. As much as anyone genuinely enjoyed a job. It had its upsides and downsides. The sales pushes when the company needed more clients. The struggling times surrounding economic hardships. The sales managers who came and went but trying to make a name for themselves. They rode along with Cal to learn the industry, and tried to find things to change. The best ones let Cal be Cal, and he responded with sales growth over time. Work was work, and he felt like he was going to be doing the same things for a long time.

Several years ago, he had applied for a sales manager position. He had prepared himself thoroughly and had some great, simple, and low-cost ideas to help sales representatives increase their sales. He drove to Atlanta for his scheduled appointment. Arrived thirty minutes early. Had extra copies of his resume and his plan of action to grow the region by twenty percent in three years.

His name was called, and Cal was guided down a long, white-walled corridor to a conference room. Inside sat a vice president Cal had met only once before at a training seminar, and the regional sales manager from Texas, Peter Woods. Peter was a great guy, and he and Cal had spent many days together over the last couple years at events and training seminars, and of course at the hotel bars afterward. Cal respected Peter because he had come from the sales side. He was a sales rep in Dallas and had done very well. His hard work had been parlayed into a regional manager position. Now he spent time in the Texas region but also training new region heads with little to no experience. Something which was happening very frequently now.

Cal was greeted warmly, and everyone shook hands as Cal took his seat across from the Vice President of Sales. His name was Don or Dan, he could not remember. He was no longer with the company, so Cal did not care to remember his name. He began speaking in a very boisterous and very southern aristocratic manner.

"Cal, thanks for coming in," he said.

"Thanks for having me," Cal said.

"Cal, this is merely a formality. We wanted to give you an interview because you are one of the best salespeople in the whole company. But I cannot give you the job. We have never had someone of your tenure in the company, nor your sales successes. Year after year, you succeed where others fail."

Cal looked confused and said, "That's a bad thing?"

"No, no, no, you misunderstand me," said Don/Dan. "We can't take our best salespeople and move them into management. We would collapse as a company. We need you on the front lines, son."

Cal asked another question. "Are you telling me, because I have been too successful, I am never going to be eligible for advancement with the company?"

"Well, no, I wouldn't say that," said Don/Dan. "This is just not the right timing for such a move."

Cal was stunned, but more important at this point, he was angry. All his hard work with the company. The long hours. The constant travel. All of it had led to this point in his career. This was his stepping-stone moment, and it was being denied him. How could this be happening? His world was crashing down around him in an instant. The mantras of the old sales guys, of training seminars, or previous managers all stated the same thing. Work hard and move up. Was it all a big lie?

He saw the irony of the moment. He was being held back for being the best. Everything in his career up until this point told him this was an impossibility. Successful people moved up. They did not get passed over.

The whole experience had irrevocably soured his faith in companies and stability. The thought of trusting a company to take care of employees or to not sell out for cash left a horribly sour taste in his mouth. The ups and downs of corporate business.

Cal had snapped back to reality and was staring at himself in the mirror.

The unpleasantness he felt six months after that horrible day. JCC had been sold. The horrible feeling was still there in the pit of his stomach. Almost twelve years with a company that no longer existed. Twelve years of his identity in a moment, with the signing of paperwork, erased for all time.

He imagined his life would continue with much of the same repeating schedule forever. He would see his sister's family on weekends and watch the kids grow until they were in college. He would work and travel every week but without the opportunity of any real advancement. Maybe find someone new to love, maybe not. He was disheartened and discouraged about life. He wanted out of this rat race.

He had no wife, no children, and no prospects. He needed something to change, and it had. Now he had the greatest of all catalysts. Money.

Money. Just thinking about the money brought a smile to his face. But there was a problem. What to do with it, and how to utilize it.

Would he rather have a place in the islands or just travel around? He could do both. Drifting around the Caribbean half the year on a boat and the other half spending time with family and friends.

He had started to spend the money in his mind. It was the greatest feeling knowing that the money was going to change his life dramatically.

He had already developed the beginnings of a plan. The plan was to continue working in his job for the next several months. Then he would offer his letter of resignation and claim an illness.

He would start taking trips to the islands for his health. There, he would open an offshore bank account and deposit the money. He needed to research how to move the money from bank to bank. Wire transfers, Swiss and Cayman bank accounts, all these things needed to be understood.

Could he really show up in the islands with two giant bags of money and walk into a bank with it? He had it all planned out in his mind. Starting with the bank. He would walk right up to the counter and ask to speak with the bank manager about a large cash deposit. He would be escorted to a luxurious wood-paneled office where a beautiful assistant would ask him if he would like some coffee or tea.

He would leave the bank a rich and free man. No debts or jobs to deal with. No headaches to deal with. He was completely unencumbered, and he was smiling.

He would start looking for his own beach house soon, but first he would enjoy the hospitality of the island as well as the night life. Also, he would enjoy the thrill of having money. The new account could buy him a house, a boat, or whatever he wanted. He might even find love and romance with a beautiful tourist and start a family. Everything was back on the table for Cal. There were no limitations when you had money. Cash is king and Cal was now a king.

He snapped out of his dream. Staring into the mirror, he looked exhausted.

The next question of his plan was, sell his little house or keep it? Obviously, it would be best to keep the house until after he could move the money. Any new owners would want to explore the fields and old property down in the valley.

Getting the money out of the barn and into the islands, or any bank account, was going to be a problem. However, that problem was months down the road.

He was tired, so he took the initiative to get a good night's sleep tonight.

Cal turned off the bathroom light and moved into the bedroom. He put on a pair of shorts and climbed into bed. Daisy followed him to her spot on a dog bed by the bedroom door.

He reached over to the nightstand and plugged in his cell phone and turned off the light.

Chapter 10

Daisy's ears popped up and her head lifted. She had heard something. She started a low growl that woke Cal from his twenty minutes of hard sleep.

"What is it, girl?" he said.

She pointed toward the window, her head not moving. Then she let out a long and loud barking that would not cease.

Cal grabbed the bat he kept next to his bed and walked down the hallway following the darting dog. Daisy was at the back door and going wild. Something was making enough noise in the backyard to get Daisy excited.

"Better not be another skunk, girl," he whispered.

He flipped on the outside lights but saw nothing.

Daisy was barking aggressively while pawing at the back door. She wanted out. Cal saw no sign of people, coyotes, or skunks. He saw nothing, so he opened the door and she darted out toward the shed.

He stepped out to follow her. He had made it about ten steps when the surge hit him. At first, he thought he had been hit by lightning. The shock was intense, and it was emanating from his back. His knees collapsed and then he heard the yelping. Daisy was crying out in pain. He wanted to run to her, to grab her and run, but he could not even raise his arms. He was on the ground shaking, staring up at a man in black. Then he passed out.

When Cal woke up, it was a slow, groggy, and painful awakening. He looked around sluggishly and tried to move, but he was tied to one of his kitchen chairs. His wrists were aching, and it felt like he was tied up with electrical wire. He looked around and saw two of his lamps were broken on the floor. Their electrical cords were missing.

"You gave him too much," said the man in black.

"I only hit him twice," said the other. "He's coming out of it."

Cal felt blood trickling down his back, and his shirt was wet. Was it blood or sweat?

Cal rolled his neck up and said, "Where is my dog?"

"See, he's OK," said the second man.

Cal asked loudly now, "What do you want? Where is my dog?"

The first man walked up and smacked Cal across the face with the back of his hand. Cal's head lurched back in surprise. A small trickle of blood started from the side of Cal's mouth.

"I'll be asking the questions tonight, Mr. Wilson," said the man in black. "Where is it?"

The first man turned to the other. "Keep searching. I'll handle this," he told him in hushed tones.

"What are you talking about?" asked Cal. "What do you want?"

"We are here for the bags. We know you have them, so tell us where they are and you won't get hurt," said the man in black.

Cal stared at him and asked, "Bags? I don't know what you are talking about."

The first man smacked him again, but harder. There were sounds coming from the rest of the house. It sounded like closets opening and items being thrown around. This was a small house. No basement. It would not take them long to search the whole place. Two giant bags would be easy to see.

Then the man in black punched Cal hard in the stomach.

"Ow, what do you want?" cried Cal.

"We know you have the bags somewhere, just tell us where they are," said the soothing voice of the man in black.

He was a big man, well over six feet tall. The other man was even bigger and wider.

Cal responded, "What bags?"

A fist came this time and hit him in the left side, upper ribs. He cried out.

"The bags," came the response from the man in black. "We can do this all night."

Blood was running down Cal's face, and his ribs were screaming in pain. Swelling was starting, and Cal was getting a little light-headed. He looked up after catching his breath. He was leaning forward almost falling out of the chair.

"Help me out here, I don't understand," cried Cal.

The next blow hit in the kidney area. The pain was intense. Cal could not breathe. He bent forward as far as his hands allowed. The pain was shooting through his body now. His whole body was sore from the taser shots, and now every blow had a heightened response. The next blow was another backhand to the right eye, and Cal fell back into the chair.

Cal was quiet. And woozy now. He was mumbling something.

The man in black leaned in to hear him better.

"Please tell me," he begged. "What do you want?"

Cal was starting to weaken now. Pain was a great motivator. It was motivating him towards giving up the money. How much more could he take, and how long could he hold out?

"The bags," came the response.

Cal stayed quiet. Each response he had given resulted in a beating. He thought, why not just stay quiet?

Another rib shot followed about five seconds of silence. Cal lost his breath again. This guy could throw a punch and knew the best places to hit him.

Cal gasped for air, and the pain erupted again.

The other man made his way into the living room, and Cal could see him out of the corner of his eye. He moved furniture and looked behind cabinets.

The man in black next to him paused for a second to check on the status of the search. Cal watched as he made his way into the living room.

This was a welcome break. Cal needed to catch his breath, and he needed a way out of this mess. How was he going to get out of this? If he told them where the money was, he was dead. If he told them nothing, he was dead. If he tried to run, he was dead.

Where was Daisy, was she alive? Had they killed her? He started to tear up now. Not from the beating, but from the thought of his loyal best friend lying dead in the yard. Focus, he thought, you will be lying there soon if you do not find a way out of this.

If he told them it was the gang, would he survive? Unknown. Cal needed to live, but how? All those piles of glorious money would rot down in the barn. What a waste. If he died right now, no one would find the money. No one would ever find the money. He did not have the money. The money was not on his property. If these guys were gang members, they would search everything and see he did not have them.

However, these were not gang members. Their speech was of white southern men, soft accent, but easily recognizable. Keep up the story. No bags. No bags. Hopefully, they will leave him alive.

The man in black came back into the dining room, and the other man went outside. Cal assumed to check around the house or cars.

The man in black walked up to Cal and bent down slowly in front of his face.

"The bags," he said.

"I don't know about any…" Cal started to say when a fist landed on his cheek.

Cal went flying back in the chair.

Another blow came from the right and caught him on the chin. Then his ribs started exploding in pain with each shot being landed. Cal slumped in the chair, motionless. The pain was excruciating, and he was starting to see black spots in his vision, and then his vision narrowed. He was looking at the floor, but there were black walls on either side of his view. He was almost unconscious.

The man left and went outside. The two men entered a minute or five later, and Cal had gone in and out of consciousness.

"It's not here," said one on the men. "We looked everywhere. Even the Jeep. It's not here."

"He'd have given it up anyway," said the other. "I roughed him up good. Look at him."

They walked over to Cal slowly. The attacker leaned down in front of the flopping head.

"The bags," said the man in black again.

Cal was just mumbling now. Not really saying anything.

"I don't..." Cal started to say when the blow caught him in the stomach and the pain rushed up his spine.

The final blow to Cal's head occurred as the man in black was walking past him. He was slumped over in the chair, his hands tied tight underneath. His jaw exposed. The final blow landed on Cal's jaw and caused him and the chair to hit the floor. The wooden chair bent and snapped under Cal's weight. Cal had finally passed out completely and lay bleeding on the hardwood floor. The men left the house after a last cursory scan of the kitchen and headed out the back door.

Cal eventually woke up with his face pressed hard against the floor. Blood was pooled around his head, and a sharp pain was building in his ribs and jaw.

He tried to move but felt his hands beneath his body. They were still tied together, and the chair was awkwardly digging into his side.

He slowly lifted his head. The pain was intense and throbbing.

He lowered it back down to the floor. He closed his eyes and began listening for any sounds of the intruders. The man in black had been short on words, but his intentions were clear. He wanted the bags.

He needed to get free of these bindings and call for help.

He wiggled his legs and arms in small motions at first. All seemed good with his legs. He rolled over on his stomach. The pain in his ribs was severe and growing steadily worse. He knew from the way it felt, he had broken his ribs.

With his hands still under what remained of the chair, Cal quickly pulled his arms under him and under his legs and the remnants of the chair legs. The pain was heavy and caused him to cry out. Shooting bolts of pain, like lightning, passed through his rib cage. He jerked back and forth until finally his hands were free from the chair. He fell back to the floor and rolled onto his back. He lay there breathing heavily for a while. When he had regained his breath and felt less sick, he crawled over to the table and pulled himself upright. He walked through the kitchen holding his side and making sure he did not fall. He turned and started down the hallway towards his bedroom. He made it to the bed and sat next to his nightstand. He reached out and grabbed his cell phone.

Do I call 911? Of course, this is another test, a guilty person might run. Take the money and run. Do not go back to the money. No unusual behavior. It would be very unusual to have a home invasion and not report it to the police.

He did not want the police here. He did not want to go to a hospital. What he wanted to do was lie here on his bed and get some rest. He just needed to sleep. His head was pounding now.

No, I need to report it. He opened the phone and dialed 911. He stood and walked toward the front door. It was still open. He closed it and locked the deadbolt. He then went to the back door.

"Daisy," he cried.

The female voice came on the phone. "911, what is your emergency?"

"My name is Calvin Wilson, 5445 Windy Hill Road, Springdale, I just had a home invasion."

"Are you hurt?" asked the operator.

"Yes," said Cal with a hard cough.

She asked a second question. "Are the suspects still there?"

"No, I don't think so," Cal said in hushed tones. He really didn't know.

"Can you describe your injuries?" the operator asked.

Cal was fighting to stay awake. His voice was hoarse and full of grit but he continued.

"They tied me to a chair and beat me," he said.

"I have dispatched units to your house and an ambulance. Stay with me on the phone," the operator said.

"They might have..." said Cal. "I think they killed my dog." Cal was starting to ramble on. He was holding the phone to his ear, but he was not aware of it.

"I'm going outside to check on my dog," said Cal.

"No, do not leave your home," said the operator. "I repeat, do not go outside. I have dispatched a unit and an ambulance. Lock the doors and wait for the unit to arrive."

There were protocols to follow, and the first one said for the unit on scene to secure the property. Do a search. The suspects were long gone, but protocol was protocol.

She asked again, "Do you understand, Mr. Wilson? Can you hear me?"

Cal had locked the door but was staring at the shed. He could not see Daisy, but he knew she was dead. Daisy would have been at the back door otherwise.

Cal slid down the wall next to the door and sat on the floor with his back to the door. He was staring across the kitchen and the living room. He was staring at the front window and waiting for blue lights to appear.

He passed out.

"Mr. Wilson," came the voice from the phone. The phone had fallen off his leg and was sitting on the floor next to him. "Can you hear me, Mr. Wilson?"

The 911 operator made a note and sent an update to the units arriving. The first unit was still five minutes out.

The sirens woke him up. He heard them as they approached the house and saw blue lights flashing in his driveway. The ambulance came around the corner, and the red and white lights were now shining across the lawn in a sea of red, white, and blue.

"Police, Mr. Wilson, are you there?" came the voice from outside the door.

"Yes," Cal said softly, but tried it again with more air.

The voice came again. "Sir, can you open the door?"

Cal tried to stand. The fogginess and the pain were a horrible combination.

Cal sat back down and said, "I am by the back door. Come to the back."

"Stay where you are, we are coming around," came the voice again.

A moment later, a voice was at the back door. "Mr. Wilson, can you open this door?"

Cal reached up and unlocked the door but still sat on the floor. He rolled onto his side and out of the way of the door opening.

The officer leaned down and looked at him. Then he rushed over and opened the front door. Two EMTs rushed in and he directed them to the kitchen.

The EMTs started checking Cal over and asking questions. Cal said, "My ribs and my face."

Then he passed out again.

The next thing Cal saw were flashes. The inside of an ambulance, the entrance to the hospital, and a light in his eyes. Then sleep.

Chapter 11

C al woke up the next day with his sister and her husband sleeping in his hospital room. One was on the couch and the other was in what looked like an extremely uncomfortable chair.

"Poor Ben," said Cal. He was slowly lifting his head. He felt nothing. He was completely numb. These must be the good drugs, he thought.

Jennifer lifted her head and looked at Cal. She was stretched out on the couch with the sunshine from the window casting shadows across her blanket covered body.

"What?" Jen asked.

"Ben looks so uncomfortable," said Cal with a hint of a slur.

She was tearing up now. "How do you feel?" she asked.

"I don't feel anything," Cal said.

"That's good, because you are not looking so good," she said.

"Well, I feel fine. Give me a kiss, sis," he demanded.

She bent down and kissed him softly on the forehead.

Jennifer sat next to him on the bed and asked, "Do you need anything?"

"Water," said Cal.

She reached over and grabbed a plastic cup with a curved straw. She gingerly placed the straw on his lips and held it in front of him. Cal slowly sipped the water and drank the whole cup.

"Thanks, sis," Cal said with a hoarse and groggy voice. "You missing being a nurse?"

"I get plenty of practice with the kids," she said with a smile. "With four, there is always one needing treatment."

Ben woke up to the sounds of voices. "Cal, buddy, you OK?" he asked. He was scrambling to his feet and heading for the bed to stand next to Jennifer.

"I'm OK, you looked worse on that chair," Cal said.

"I don't think you have seen a mirror yet," said Ben.

Jennifer smacked him in the chest. "Shut up, Ben, this is not the time," she said.

"Sorry, honey," Ben said. "What did happen, Cal? The police said it was a home invasion. I went by your place to lock up and get you some clothes."

Cal asked, "Did you see Daisy?"

"Sorry, buddy," Ben started and stuttered. "She's dead. Cops think she was hit by a taser. No blood, just a burn mark. I buried her in your yard this morning. Nurses said you must stay here a while, so I did not want to leave her in the yard with the coyotes around."

"Poor Daisy," Cal said. "She didn't deserve that."

"I'm sorry, buddy," said Ben. "She was a good friend. The kids loved her too, we all did."

Cal was tearing up a little. "Thanks, Ben, I really owe you one," said Cal.

"No worries, I know you would do the same for me and more," said Ben. "I locked up your place, but it will take some time to get it cleaned up and back to its normal, pristine, non-child destroyed shape. Jen and I are planning to go clean it tonight. They destroyed the place looking for valuables."

"Don't worry about it," said Cal. "I'll take care of it."

"No, it will take both of us a while to get it back together," said Ben. "Your computer is missing, and who knows what else."

Cal looked puzzled and asked, "My computer?"

"Don't worry, it's all replaceable," added Jennifer.

"Tell me about the kids," said Cal. "Let's change the subject."

The three of them spent the next half hour discussing gymnastics, travel ball, school, teachers, and Ben's work as a lawyer in a small Atlanta firm.

The nurse broke up the discussion and said, "Can we have the room?" She was smiling and happy Cal was awake, but now she needed to do some follow-up tests.

Cal said, "I am getting pretty tired."

"We'll go get some lunch and come back," said Ben. "Do you want us to bring you anything?"

"I would love a coffee," said Cal.

"You got it, buddy," said Ben.

Ben and Jennifer left the room, and the nurse started checking his vitals. The day progressed slowly, like all hospital visits did.

***

In the early evening, Ben and Jen prepared to leave the hospital. They needed a break and some fresh air. The nurses needed to take care of Cal, and everyone was tired. They needed to get out of this sterile and white-walled hospital. Obviously, the vending machine had not provided enough sustenance, so they headed out to get some dinner, work on the house, and start preparing an itinerary of items potentially missing or damaged in the incident. They said goodbye to Cal and made their way out of his room.

They walked through the hospital in silence. They wandered on through the winding maze of corridors, encountering many sets of double doors, then they found a light green line on the floor which led them to their garage and out the last set of doors.

Jen asked, "Why are hospitals designed like prisons?"

"I guess to keep in the patients," said Ben.

They walked toward their car. It had been sitting for almost ten hours in the same spot.

"I'm starving," exclaimed Ben. "What do you want to eat?"

"Me too," said Jen. "I feel like tacos, let's get them to go and eat at Cal's house."

Ben pushed the button on the key fob and the doors unlocked to their three-year-old, gray Chevrolet Suburban. With a family of six, a large SUV was a must-have. The cost did not matter; it was a requirement. This gas guzzling beast sat six kids easily and allowed for friends or grandparents to tag along.

Now Ben was negotiating it out of a hospital garage parking space. They drove down the garage ramps and out the exit, stopping to pay seven dollars in parking fees at the booth.

Ben asked, "Taco Bell or Del Taco?"

"They don't have Del Taco here," said Jen. "I think there is a Taco Bell in Springdale. Let's go there."

"OK, I need about a dozen tacos, a walk, and a gallon of Mountain Dew," Ben said with a chuckle. She stared at him with a look of contempt.

"Really," she said.

"For sure," he said. "Hell of a day, and I'm guessing we will be up all night. Cal's place is a wreck. After I dropped you at the hospital this morning, remember, I had to go to the house," he said. "After I buried Daisy, I looked around. Everything is moved, opened, and thrown around. Even the carpets on the floor are lifted. Like they were looking for a hidden room."

"You do deserve a big meal, I forgot about your work this morning," she said. "However, how about a half-gallon of Mountain Dew?"

"No deal," he said. He leaned over and smirked at her.

"You idiot," she said.

"I need the energy," he said. "Are we headed back to the hospital tonight? Cal looked tired."

Ben wanted to stay at the house and let Cal get some rest, but Jen was in sister mode, which just so happened to be mom mode as well. She was in charge and Ben was the muscle. A relationship that had worked for their fourteen years of marriage.

"It's 8:15 pm, we should probably let him rest," she said.

"Good idea," he replied. "We can head over early in the morning. They are supposed to release him anyway, tonight is just a precaution."

They drove for twenty more minutes before reaching the Taco Bell. They ordered large amounts of tacos, burritos, and nachos and headed for Cal's little house.

They pulled into the driveway at 8:49 pm, and Ben left the car running.

"Do you want to eat inside or right here?" he asked.

"Inside, of course," she said.

"Just so you know, it's a mess, and you will want to clean up before you eat," he said. "That is not possible."

"I'm too hungry for that," she said.

They gathered the food bags up, and Ben turned off the engine and headed toward the front door, stepping on the paver stones in the yard which led to the front porch. Ben turned the key in the door and switched on the light. Jen was shocked.

"It's horrible," she said.

They were standing in the living room which contained an upside down sofa, overturned chairs, and moved cabinets. Every door and drawer was open. Nothing was untouched. Items belonging to Cal were everywhere.

Cal was exceptionally clean and organized. He believed in only keeping things he would use, so Jen knew she would not find piles of useless paperwork and old mail. Some of the items on the floor were dog food, dog toys, scissors, tape, batteries, remote controls, souvenirs, framed photos, books, and DVDs.

"Let's go to the table," said Ben.

He walked ahead and switched on the lights. Cal's modern gray walls and black furniture came to life, just not in the same places as before.

They made their way across the mess and into the dining room. There, the table and chairs were upright except for one broken one. A small pool of blood was on the floor next to the broken chair.

"Have a seat," said Ben. "Let's just eat."

Ben found a hand towel on the sink and draped it across the floor, covering the blood.

They sat down and started to tear open the bags of food containing tacos, nachos, and burritos, along with the sauces and napkins that always accompanied every order.

After a long period of silence, except for a few chewing sounds, finally Ben spoke. "We need a plan of attack, what do you want to work on?"

"Kitchen and living room," she said.

"OK, I'll head to the back rooms," he said. "First, I'll take care of this mess in here."

Jen looked at the blood on the floor. She nodded.

Ben oversaw cataloging the household items. This was because of his personality and the fact that he was the only organized member of the family. He felt he could help his brother-in-law most in this aspect. He did not want him returning to the scene of the crime and reliving this horror all over again.

The two of them worked diligently to clean and pick up the mess. Ben started by hard scrubbing the bloodstains out of the hardwood floors. Jen worked in the kitchen putting everything back into cabinets, throwing away broken dishes, and running the dishwasher. When that task was done, she moved into the living room to focus on straightening the furniture.

Ben moved down the hall and started working in the two bedrooms. He put the mattress and box springs back on the bed frame. He stripped the sheets off the bed and took them to the laundry room. He put them in the washing machine, put in the laundry soap, which was strategically placed above the washer, and closed the lid.

Ben hated folding clothes but proceeded to move all the clothes from the floor to the bed. His plan was to solicit Jen to help him after he had finished the rest of the room.

Three hours later, the house was mostly restored. There were many broken items. Ben had taken pictures, created a spreadsheet, and estimated their value. He had also added the missing computer to the list.

To Ben, this whole burglary seemed strange. He did not know all the items taken, or if there was cash or jewelry somewhere, but to his knowledge, Cal did not keep these types of things.

Then Jen called out to him from the kitchen. "Ben, get in here," she said.

Ben walked down the hallway to find Jen holding a black trash bag. It appeared as if nothing was inside.

Ben asked, "What's up?"

"Take a look at this, please," she said. She handed him the bag and walked to the living room window and closed the blinds and curtains.

Ben opened the bag and said, "Whoa."

"We need to talk to my brother," she said.

***

Outside in the same clearing near the farm entrance sat a police cruiser. There was no one inside. Standing in the field about a quarter mile from the vehicle stood Officer Denny. He was using field binoculars and watching Cal's house intently. He knew the family had left the hospital, and he assumed they would come here to pick up the money. His plan was to watch them and let them empty the hiding space he was unable to find the night before. He had been watching and waiting. Luckily, this was a slow night in Springdale, and Collins was covering for him on watch.

Cal's computer web search results made it clear; Cal had the money. He was searching for the gang shootout, counterfeit money, and money laundering.

This was taking too long. Collins texted him several times asking what was going on. The answer was nothing. The family was cleaning the house. Why would they waste their time cleaning the house? Get the money, head out, and let me pull you over, he thought.

After an hour, Denny went back to the warmth and comfort of the police cruiser. He would stay for a while longer, but this lead was going nowhere. Cal had obviously not shared his secret with his sister. If he had the money.

This guy had the money somewhere.

When Cal got out the hospital, they were going to find out where. If they had to follow him for a week, they would find the money. He would lead them to bags. Collins came over the radio, and the trade-off started. Denny started the car and left the drive, headed for town. They passed each other on Windy Hill.

Collins drove slowly past the house, and as he did, the window curtains snapped closed. He was in for a long night of waiting.

***

Ben looked shocked. He asked, "What is this?"

"It's sixty thousand dollars, Ben!"

"Holy shit," he said. "Where was it?"

"In the bottom of the garbage can, under a bag of trash," Jen exclaimed. "Why would he have sixty thousand dollars in the bottom of the garbage can?"

"Maybe he hates banks," said Ben with a smirk and a giggle.

Jen started to look mad. "What the hell is wrong with him?"

"There may be a reasonable, yet odd explanation for this," Ben said.

"Ben, do you think he could be in some kind of trouble?"

"I would normally say no in regard to your brother, he is too boring," Ben said.

Jen asked, "Normally?"

"When you take into account the state of this place and the fact that Cal is hiding the money in the last place anyone would look, and we know because they looked everywhere," said Ben.

Jen was worried now. Her face was sinking, and her eyes were wide. Her heart was racing, and she needed to think. She walked over to the newly flipped over couch and fell into it. She asked, "Not a coincidence?"

"I'm a lawyer, I don't believe in coincidences," said Ben.

She looked up at him and asked, "What did he do?"

"I have no idea," Ben said. "I know you don't carry sixty grand in cash around. It is too dangerous. There are people in this world that will kill you for what you have in your pocket. Sixty thousand dollars is just too enticing."

"So, he was lucky to survive this whole thing and walk away," she said.

"My guess is he was beaten to get him to talk about the money," he said. "When he did not, they either assumed he didn't know anything or he didn't have the money anymore. He has three broken ribs, taser burns, and lots of bruises. They worked him over trying to find out."

"Find out what?" she exclaimed.

"That is what we need to ask him tomorrow," he said. "I'm tired, help me get the sheets on the bed, and let's get up early and find out."

Jen yawned and looked at him. "Did you call the kids?"

"I did, they were already asleep, but your mom said they were great and she had no issues," he said. "We can call them over breakfast."

"Let's get those sheets out of the dryer," said Jen.

"Already on the bed," he said with a smirk.

"You tease, you know how much I hate putting sheets on the bed," she said. "You do love me."

"I better, we have a whole litter together," he said.

They walked into the bathroom and each took a shower and made their way toward the newly cleaned up bedroom. The gray walls and black furniture in the bedroom seemed almost like a hotel to them. Their home was in constant disarray, and they lacked any sort of style or cohesion. Much of their furniture had been gathered during the law school years from Goodwill or other students moving away. They could never understand how people could create cohesive living spaces or have the disposable income to have matching items.

***

When Jen got out of the shower, she walked naked and semi-dry into the bedroom, where Ben was already lying on top of the sheets in his boxers.

"Hey, wake up," she said. "Let's pull back the sheets."

Ben slowly rolled off the side of the bed and pulled back the sheets. They both climbed in and sat in silence for a while. Ben had easily drifted back to sleep. His soft repetitious breathing was the key indicator.

Jen was having a hard time falling asleep. Her mind was racing, and she was asking herself many questions she did not know the answers to. What was Cal involved with? Why was there so much cash in his house? Were the people who did this coming back?

She suddenly felt very vulnerable. She eased out of bed and grabbed one of Cal's T-shirts from the basket of freshly folded laundry and put in on.

She went to the living room and started checking all the door locks. Kitchen door, garage door, and front door. All locked. She turned off the lights and eased to the front window. The curtains had been drawn since she'd found the money. She stuck her head through the break in the curtains and let her eyes adjust to the outside. She was just starting to think how silly she was being when she caught a slight movement out of the corner of her eye. She focused on the area and watched as a shadow walked down the edge of the road and away from the house. The moon was out bright, and she could just make out the shape of a policeman.

Why was a policeman walking in the field across from the house?

She stood very still, hoping he would not see her head. He was getting further from the house now.

"What you looking at?"

"Jesus! Don't scare me, you ass!" she said.

"Just wondering where you were," he said.

She took a couple deep breaths and said, "Look out there. There is a cop walking around in the field, watching the house. Did they say they were going to do that?"

"No, and I doubt they knew we were even going to stay here," he said. "I never told them."

"Why is he out there?"

Ben stuck his head around the curtains. "Where is he?"

"To the left, heading toward that old driveway," she said.

"Oh, I see him," he said. "It is a cop."

"Maybe they are just checking on the house," she said.

"They would pull into the driveway and do a perimeter check if that was their interest," he said. "This is something else."

"What?"

"I don't know," he said. "This is odd behavior, and it would seem like they are spying on us."

"You don't think…"

"No, maybe, I don't know," he said. "We don't know what is going on, but one thing is for sure. Someone thinks we do."

Jen left the window and walked over to the counter where the garbage bag full of stacked bills sat.

"Let's put this back where we found it for now," she said.

"Good idea, the last thing we need is to get caught with that money," he said.

Jen folded the garbage back up into a tight bundle and placed it under the current trash bag, which was new and not full of old take-out. Ben had taken out the trash earlier.

"Let's try to get some sleep," she said.

Ben was still staring out of the window.

"I think he is heading to his vehicle," he said. "Yes, headlights."

Jen ran over to the window.

"Let me see," she said.

Ben made room and both of their heads were now on the other side of the curtains.

The headlights were shining upwards and then pointed down to the road. They slowly turned to the left and headed toward the house. The car was moving slowly, and Ben and Jen had plenty of time to get a good look before darting inside of the curtains.

"Springdale Police," he said.

The car moved past the house and down the road. When Ben poked his head out again. The car's red taillights were moving along quickly in the distance.

"To bed," he said. "We can figure this out in the morning."

It took about twenty minutes, but they both finally drifted off to sleep.

Chapter 12

Cal awoke to a nurse changing out his IV bag. His eyes were heavy, and the drugs were working their way through his system. He looked up at the nurse and around his hospital room. He saw a whiteboard with nurse's notes on them, a television on a stand near the ceiling, and some maple-colored cabinets on the wall most likely filled with room supplies. He leaned his head over to the right and saw his private bathroom.

"Excuse me, Nurse," he said. "I need to use the bathroom; can you help me up?"

"Sure, hon," said the nurse.

Her name was Janet. It was written on the board. Cal had seen his shift nurses' names on that board for the last day.

Janet walked over and helped Cal ease upward slowly. She was a woman in her late forties with some hard miles on her. She had a larger body frame, and at five foot nine, she looked as though she had been a beauty in her prime. That prime was most likely fifteen years ago, and now she had bad skin, a couple small liver spots, and a short haircut dyed light blonde. The one thing she possessed that was easy to remember was her smile. It was cute, small, and thin-lined. She was always smiling and had a very pleasant demeanor.

Janet moved to the right side of the bed, closest to the bathroom. She approached Cal and made sure to pull the IV stand close to the bed. She then removed the blankets and helped him turn his legs to the edge of the bed. Cal slowly stood up and placed his feet on the ground. He was happy to see that his legs held up.

He grunted a bit at first, but moving around was making him feel a little better, not just a helpless patient. Janet stood with him to the bathroom, and he sat down on the toilet.

"Just holler when you are finished," she said.

"Thank you," said Cal.

Cal relieved himself for an exceedingly long time. The benefit of all the IV bags was a complete bodily fluid cleanse, he thought. The drugs were still in his system, even though they had reduced the amount the night before. The doctor told him he would be fine; no permanent damage and the MRI was clear. No swelling in the brain. Just some broken ribs, bruises, and cuts on his wrists and face.

Cal could hear the assailant in his mind. "The bags," he heard repeatedly.

He wanted to get out of the hospital as soon as he could, but what then? Home was not safe. They had searched everywhere for the money but had come up empty. They were not going to give up. Whoever they were. They had two million reasons to keep coming back.

Cal was beating himself up about his computer. Why had he not erased the search history? He could explain away the interest in the shootout, but the money searches, that was a tough one. How to determine if your money is counterfeit, and even a search of how to launder money. These were some incriminating searches, and the attackers would be back. They had his computer and they would know this by now. He could not go home. He needed a plan. A place to go and hide. Home. I hope Jen and Ben did not go there last night. They need to stay away from me and this whole thing.

I need to get away and hide in a jungle somewhere, he thought. Now where can I find a jungle?

In Cal's youth, he had been an avid backpacker and hiker. He still loved hiking but had not been in a couple years, outside of a walk down a greenway with Jen and the kids on a Saturday afternoon.

"Backpacking," he said.

His mind was still a little foggy, but he was trying to remember some of the places he had gone when he was in his college years. Places where there were no power lines, roads, people. Some of the most beautiful collages of scenery popped into his mind. Mountain tops, river valleys, and long winding trails. All great places to hide, but for how long? Most of the places were remote but were mostly part of day hikes. It would be hard to hide out on those hikes. Park rangers and other hikers would be prevalent.

I need to hide out for months and come back for the money after things die down, he thought. I don't want to leave the country. I want to stay close by and try to develop a plan to hide and move the money, but also develop a plan on how to be able to use it.

The sixty thousand dollars came to mind. If he could survive on the money for the next several months, he might be able to stay off the grid for a while. He would need to pay his mortgage and bills. Maybe Ben could help with that. He could give him some cash, and Ben could make the payments for him.

The plan was starting to come together. He needed to get out of town fast. He was Calvin Wilson here. He needed a fresh start and a new name. Springdale was not safe for him. He needed to leave quickly.

"You OK in there?" said Janet with a tone of concern.

"All good," he said. "I'm finished."

He reached behind and flushed the toilet.

Janet came in and helped him to his feet.

"Any pain?" she asked.

"Just sore," he said.

"Good," she said. "You are being discharged today. Do you have someone who can help you till you're healed up?" she asked.

"Yes, family," he said. "They should be here soon."

"Good," she said with a smile. "It's nice to have family to help you in times like this."

"For sure," he said. "Can I get dressed now?"

"I don't see why not," said Janet. "Let me get your clothes. Just sit here on the edge of the bed and I will help you get them on."

Janet gathered the clothes from a plastic bag hanging on the back of the door and helped Cal slowly ease his aching bones and muscles out of the hospital gown and into the jeans, tee shirt, socks, and tennis shoes. These were new. Not items he had worn into the hospital.

Ben, he thought. Jen is a lucky girl; Ben is always on top of things.

Cal looked up at Janet and asked, "Where are the clothes I came in with?"

"They are in evidence," she said. "In an assault situation, the crime lab gathers the clothes to search for DNA or evidence of the attacker."

"My brother-in-law would have known that, and hence he brought me new clothes," he said.

"Police officer?"

"Lawyer, but a really good guy," Cal said.

Janet laughed a little chuckle and finished easing the Metallica tee shirt over Cal's bruised and bandaged ribs.

"There," she said. "All set. Now just sit here on the bed until we are ready to discharge you. The doctor will be by shortly, and I am sure your family will be here soon. Push the buzzer if you need anything."

She walked around to the other side of the bed and moved the roller cart with a tray of food on it until it crossed over Cal's waist.

"Eat up," she said. "I'll be in with some ibuprofen in a little while."

"Thank you, Janet," he said.

***

Ben woke up around six thirty. The sounds of the birds tweeting and a distant roll of thunder snapped him awake. He lay there for a moment remembering the past twenty-four hours and all the details that came together to put him in this strange bed.

He turned his head to the side and saw Jen staring at him.

"Storm's coming," she said.

"I heard it," he said.

"We need to get some answers from my brother," she said. "Let's head to Waffle House down the road for some breakfast, and then go get him at the hospital."

"Sounds perfect," he said. "Let's also pack him some clothes, shoes, and anything else he will need."

Jen looked confused. "Aren't we bringing him home?"

"We can't," Ben said with a look of serious awareness of the situation. "There are several reasons why. One, he was attacked here, and it can happen again. Two, the money makes this not a typical robbery or break-in. Three, he may not want to come back to the place where it happened so soon afterward. Most importantly, he needs to heal, and may need our help."

She looked at him with soft eyes. "Did you sleep at all?"

"A little," he said. "I was running over the scenario in my head several times during the night. It's most likely that he needs to deal with whatever this is directly, or he needs to get clear of it. Either way, he is not coming back here for a while."

"I'll gather his things," she said. "You are always two steps ahead of me."

Jen leaned in and kissed her husband on the nose. Then the lips. He kissed her back, hard. Then one thing led to another as often happens when the Browns were away from their kids for any amount of time. They wrapped themselves up in the freshly cleaned sheets and took advantage of the time to themselves.

Jen and Ben walked into Cal's hospital room around nine in the morning to find Cal rested, fed, and dressed for discharge.

"Morning, brother," Jen said.

"Hey, sis," he responded softly. "I'm ready to go."

"Sounds good," Jen said. "What did the doctor say?"

Cal coughed a little and took a drink of water.

"He came by a few minutes ago," Cal said. "He said there was no permanent damage and the MRI looked clean. He told me to rest up and call him if I started to feel lightheaded or any type of head issues. I'm good to go, so let's go."

"OK then, sounds like you love the hospital and would like to stay at least one night more," said Jen with a slight smile.

Ben was giggling under his breath.

"I'll get the nurse," Ben said.

Ben left the room and walked to the nurse's station.

"Hello there," Ben said to the nurse on duty. "My brother-in-law said he was ready to be discharged," Ben said politely. "He is in room 206."

"Mr. Wilson, yes, he is ready to go," she said. "He has signed his paperwork. All we need is your signature on this form saying you are picking him up."

"Can I borrow your pen?" asked Ben.

"Certainly," she said and handed him a cheap, blue Bic pen.

Ben quickly read over the discharge document and signed his name to the paper.

"Also, we will need copies of all his medical records to take with us," Ben said.

"I will need Mr. Wilson to sign a couple more forms, then," she said.

"We can wait," Ben said.

"You can, but I think Mr. Wilson is more than ready to hit the road," she said with a chuckle. "I'll start printing these, but let me go get his signatures. I'll be right back."

Ben leaned up against the side of the nurse's station. The well-used, cream-colored counter was clean but smelled of disinfectant. He stood up straight, grabbed his phone, and checked his email.

Being an attorney was in his blood. He thought about future problems or issues and how to deal with them well before they could cause any damage or discomfort. His boss, the executive VP, described him as being three steps ahead.

In the early days of Ben's career, and right out of law school, he worked for the district attorney's office in Atlanta. As a fresh young assistant district attorney, he was thrown to the wolves of the judicial system, and to survive, he worked eighty plus hours a week. He was a quick study and picked up the routine, the organization, and the determination to win cases.

There were about a hundred ADAs in Fulton County Office of the District Attorney, and Ben eventually stood out. He had a respectable conviction rate. The occasional high-powered drug lawyer or organized crime lawyer would get in his way and his percentages would suffer. These high-powered defense attorneys knew their stuff and could see in every discrepancy a way to create doubt and uncertainty.

He quickly earned the respect of both sides of the aisle and created great relationships with the judges as well.

After three years of obscure poverty and long hours, Ben was searching for legal jobs with better hours. It took him about three months of interviewing and searching, but he finally landed a job as a corporate attorney for an international hospitality company who had set up their North American headquarters in Atlanta. He had been there ever since. Seven years of steady hours, vacation, and good salary.

He knew many other law school buddies who had high-powered roles with two hundred to three hundred thousand dollars a year, but they were killing themselves. Divorce, alcoholism, and all kinds of vices were entrenched in their lives. Working over ninety hours a week for a life that was falling apart never interested Ben.

They had a modest four-bedroom, three-bath house in the northern suburbs of Atlanta, near his office. He did not suffer through the long commutes Atlanta was famous for. He wanted a neighborhood close to work and safe.

He currently made ninety-two thousand a year and worked about forty-five hours a week on average. He liked the work and felt lucky to have found a career and a lifestyle that suited him so well.

He knew that insurance was going to come asking about Cal's injuries. He also knew that Cal would not be back at this hospital for a while and might want to lay low. Criminal or not, Cal was a good man and, more important, he was family.

Requesting medical records would give away his location and could put him at risk. He wanted to make sure his friend and brother-in-law was safe and secure. The best way to control the outcome was to take over the decisions around Cal.

Besides, he wanted to get a full report and not get a secondhand version from Cal. He knew Jen would appreciate that as well.

"We are good," said the nurse. "He didn't even look at the forms. He is ready for the wheelchair."

She reached into the file and inserted the newly-signed documents. Then she turned to the printer and grabbed the twenty odd pages of documents and placed them in a manila envelope and handed them to Ben.

"Thanks so much," Ben said.

"Not a problem, I'll call for an orderly," she said while picking up the phone.

Ben made his way back to the room with documents in hand.

"What's that?" asked Jen.

"Your brother's life story," Ben said.

Twenty minutes later, Ben picked up Jen and Cal in front of the hospital's main doors.

Cal was moving well, and it appeared most of the heavy drugs were out of his system.

Ben pulled out of the hospital parking area and headed for the interstate. He was headed for home.

In the car, Jen blurted out, "So, what's the sixty thousand for?"

"Repairs to the house, I guess," said Cal.

Jen was staring at him from across the back seat. She was not blinking or looking away. She wanted an answer and she was going to get it.

"You know, we saw someone last night watching the house," she said.

Cal flinched first. "What?"

"Oh yes, and I bet he was hoping we would find something they were looking for," she said.

"Let's talk about it, Cal," she said.

An hour later, Jen, Ben, and Cal exited the family Suburban at a rest area on I-75. They had been heading south to Atlanta and were engrossed in Cal's recounting of the events of the last couple days.

Cal was walking gingerly, and he was grimacing, but he was moving, and the doctors assured Jen he was going to be fine.

"Do you need any help?" both asked Cal at the same time.

"You two should really stop spending so much time together," said Cal.

They smiled and hugged each other, and Jen snorted back, "We have to make up for your lack of social skills."

She smiled and continued. "Seeing anybody?"

"No, sis," Cal said. "Can you please hook me up with some of your mom group friends?"

"Not my friends," she laughed. "You will have them bothering me when you stop calling."

"True," said Cal. "Probably best if we avoid that situation."

Ben was laughing and dragging Jen toward the steps up to the glass doors. The rest area was a large and open area with pine trees all around. The brick and glass building looked like a 1980s building in true government style.

Cal was moving slowly and stretching out his muscles cautiously. In an effort not to hurt himself anymore, he was slowly making his way up the curb and onto the sidewalk.

"Look, they have a handy-capable ramp for you, bro," said Jen. "Take your time, we will meet you back at the car. Maybe you will have time to meet someone special by then."

"Ha, ha," said Cal. "Lovely, poke fun at the crippled and hobbled man."

"I'll grab you a coke at the machines," Ben said as he was climbing the stairs.

"Diet Dr. Pepper for me, babe," said Jen.

"Of course," Ben replied.

Cal made it without incident or speed through the rest area experience and back to the car. He was buckling his seat belt when Jen asked, "Why not just give them the money back?"

"Back? I did not steal it. I don't know who it belongs to," Cal snorted. "Plus, I am pretty sure everyone who was there that night is dead."

"Dead?"

Ben asked, "The marina shootout?"

"Right, it appears everyone died on the scene, as best they can tell."

"Wait," asked Jen. "Then who did this to you, and who is watching the house?"

Cal was sitting up in his seat and cringing a little. "Yesterday, I thought about it all day," he said. "I could not get it out of my mind. I fixated on it and I could only come up with three real possibilities. All really hard to verify, but I have a plan."

"Let me guess," said Jen. "The two gangs from the shootout are obvious, but the third one is tough. Their lawyer?"

Ben laughed. "Damn straight, we lawyers are gangster."

"Not the lawyer, but the law," whispered Cal.

Ben turned around and looked at him then spoke. "Are you serious?"

"I am," said Cal.

Jen started to say, "Why, would the—"

Ben and Cal both said, "Money."

Cal started explaining. "I saw a car that night fly by my place in pursuit of the other cars. At first, I thought it was another gang car. Now that I think about it, I feel they were being watched."

"By who?" asked Ben.

"Who knows, maybe the cops or FBI. They obviously knew what was in the car they were following. With that much money, everyone wanted it."

"So, you think it was cops?" asked Jen.

"I do now," said Cal. "Everyone died at the marina, so they could not find the money or get information about where it was." Cal sighed and shifted uneasily in his seat.

"You OK?" asked Jen.

"No," said Cal. "I was beaten and left for dead. The good news is I'm rich."

"Very funny, bro," Jen replied. "Do you need us to stop?"

"Please," said Cal. "Sitting like this is painful."

Ben found a coffee shop on his map program and made his way off the exit. He parked in front of the glass doors, and they slowly went inside.

Cal waited in a reading nook with a soft leather couch and two matching brown leather reading chairs.

"You were saying it was cops," Ben said, holding an Americano for Cal and handing it to him.

"Oh, that's good. I needed good coffee."

"Cal…" said Jen.

"Yeah, look, my theory is they were following the money, right? Somehow. A tracker or maybe they saw the transfer. They were far enough back to remain secret."

"OK, but the cops don't know much about what happened," said Jen. "Seems like they would know more if they had an investigation."

"Right, but what if they were not following them to bust them?" said Ben. "What if they were following them to protect them or guard them?"

"Maybe rob them," said Jenn.

"Maybe," said Cal. "Yeah. Makes sense everyone would be after the cash."

"If they were there to protect them, I don't think they would have dumped the cash in my yard."

"Good point," said Ben.

"So, what, they were there to rob them?" asked Jen again.

"I think you may be right, sis."

"Not good, Cal," said Ben. "There are no gang members left who know where the money is, and the cops are the ones looking."

"That means it was the cops who attacked you," Jen whispered. "They knew it was not at the marina. They figured it was dumped somewhere on the road. Easy to search the road afterward."

"Not a lot of houses, maybe fifteen," said Cal. "Easy to go one by one."

"They chose you," said Ben. "Why?"

"My stretch of road has a blind spot on the chase. Once you go over the hill, you would be out of sight for a few seconds. Plus, my pine trees make a good hiding place. That cop was sure interested in looking there."

"What cop?" asked Jenn.

"Oh yeah, forgot to tell you. A cop came by on Saturday. He said he was doing a routine search of the area. Said sometimes bad guys throw drugs and guns away. Not to touch the bag as it could be laced with psychedelics. Just call him."

"Definitely the cops," said Jen.

"I thought it was normal since a car chase had just gone through the area the night before and there was a shootout at the marina," said Cal. "I thought it was procedure."

"Do you know his name?" asked Ben.

"Yeah, I have his card in my wallet."

Cal maneuvered carefully to his side and pulled out his front pocket wallet. He took out the business card and handed it to Ben.

"Officer Justin Denny, Springdale Police," said Ben. "We will be on the lookout for him."

Chapter 13

J immy was wearing a black wool overcoat and gray slacks. He was a handsome man with a sharp, narrow face and brown skin. He wore a thin mustache on his lip and resembled Clark Gable in his current attire.

Jimmy, unlike most Thirteens of the past, had no exposed tattoos. Luis hated them. He told all the new initiates it was an effortless way to get noticed by the authorities or your enemies. Wearing your colors on your face was never a good decision. It was like telling the guy you're about to hit that the punch was coming. So, the unofficial rule was stealth, and he taught the new guys to never have any tattoos on the hands or face. It was a tradition of those with short life spans. Luis and Jimmy both wore their colors on their backs.

Three days had passed since his men had been killed. Luis had exhausted all his resources, and the men had been shaking the street for information.

There was none.

It was a Tuesday morning with funerals planned for Friday and Saturday. Outside it was a cold, dark, and dreary day. A light mist was falling, and the sky was gray and threatening snow.

Jimmy had made it to the shop around ten in the morning and was catching up on intel before briefing Luis. The room was well lit with all the shop lamps in the ceiling humming away. Jimmy sat at the old wood counter that had been pulled out of a closed bar in the area. He was holding a coffee cup in one hand and a disposable cell phone in the other, a small steno pad and pen in front of him. At thirty-eight years old, he was the old man in the crew. People respected Jimmy. They did not overly fear him. They should have. Not only had he killed more men than most of his soldier crews combined, his mind was quick and vengeful. But his outward exterior painted a different persona, one of a Mexican Mr. Rogers.

He had just come from Jose Martinez's mother's house where he paid his respects to the family. His wife had made a dish of chicken and mole sauce. She and her kids were at the Martinez's right now. Soon, they would take some food over to the Rodriguez home.

These families were remarkably close. Growing up in the gang and in the neighborhood afforded the chance for everyone to be close. There was truly little socializing with anyone outside the gang.

The morning so far was in full progression. The bodies had been recovered, studied by the FBI, and released to the funeral parlors for preparation of the upcoming services. Jimmy had been to both homes and delivered an eloquent and passionate call for vengeance and had prayed with the families. His touching words when describing his men had made Mrs. Martinez cry loudly, and all were in tears. He was an eloquent speaker and had a soothing calmness in his tone. The message had been brief but simple. Those that had taken from them would suffer at the hands of God, but first by his hand. The words were not hollow, and none thought they were. Jimmy was a sincere person and did what he promised. He promised all the family members he would exact a vengeance for this loss.

A call came into his cell phone and Jimmy answered.

Luis yelled at him to come over. Jimmy was about to brief Luis on operations, so he walked over while listening to his man's report and began leaning up against the light beige wood paneling near Luis's fine mahogany wood desk.

A minute passed. Then Jimmy ended the call.

"We have not been able to connect with the Russians," Jimmy said. "They are either caught in an attempt to double-cross us, or they are worried we think so."

"What about their money guys and runners here?"

"They are quiet. No movement. I think they pulled out of the city," said Jimmy.

"Smart, they know we will hit them. Best to give us no play at all."

"Luis, we need to retaliate, and quick."

"I spoke with Juan again today. I have them sitting on the casino and watching out for any Russians. We know they work out of there. No movement yet, but we will stay till they do. Speaking of which, can you get some more of those prepaid credit cards from the credit union scam and some cash up to those guys today? We need to keep a good cover going. Also, I want them in new white guy clothes, blend in. Take them shopping."

"No problem," Jimmy responded.

"Have we any new information on the chase, marina shootout, or Springdale?"

"We do, I spoke with our contacts at the local paper, and it appears like two vehicles were in a high-speed chase. They were shooting at each other and trying to get distance from one another.

"In the Russian SUV, they found a cell jammer, a radio jammer for walkie and two-way radio transmissions, and a map of prospective routes and ambush points. Looks like if our boys had stayed on the highway, they would have run into a massive ambush on the off-ramp here in town. The jammers were still on when the pigs arrived on scene. Took the FBI to figure it out. That was why the news about it is so slow developing. They never got the chance to broadcast it over the radio."

"Jimmy, they have been watching us for a while," Luis exclaimed.

"Yes, but most of it is just common sense," Jimmy relayed with a breath. "They don't know our drops, safe houses, gun stores, or money dumps. They don't know where our bookmaking or drug cutting is taking place. If they did, it would be different. They just know where our territory lines are. Most know that."

"Where is our money? We are out almost a million to the cartel for the coke. It will take us a year to get that much liquid cash again. So where is the money? If everyone died in the shootout, where is the money?"

"I've been thinking about that," Jimmy mused. He walked over and sat in the leather chairs across from the desk. "I've got three scenarios, there may be more. If we start canceling out what we know, we may be able to move in the right direction."

"Let's hear it."

"One, they figured there was an ambush coming. Jose was smart. He had his boy ditch the bags at a remote spot and planned to come back for it."

"Agree, that's where my mind goes too. Don't give the Russians an opportunity to claim the cash."

"Right. Two, there were more Russians at the marina, and they grabbed the money and ran. Unlikely since they left the bodies, phones, and guns of their comrades on the ground."

"Agreed."

"Three, the cops took it," Jimmy said with an exasperated tone. He exhaled hard. "First on the scene. A giant bag of cash. Too tempting for anyone."

"Very likely. The more I think of this option, the more it just fits. Do we know who was on the scene?"

"No," Jimmy responded. "The police reports are not being released. It is an FBI investigation, and they don't release anything."

"Don't we have a contact over there we move cash through? He tells me the mayor is bent in the right direction. Can he be spoken with?"

"Not directly," said Jimmy.

"Let's take a step back. Jimmy, this is not a large town. How many cops could they possibly have?"

"Not many."

"Let's go one by one. We can involve the right people. Let's put the tech boys on this. Create a list and we will check them off as we go. Maybe we can get lucky."

"I like it," Jimmy said. "I'll get them started. Can't be more than a couple dozen cops."

"Get some of the new kids, the initiates to the tech boys, up there in person. They must have a library or coffee shop or something for them to park in. I want everything. I want numbers of cops, unit numbers, shift changes. Anything they can get."

"We are spreading pretty thin. We have guys at the casino, we are putting guys in Springdale, and we have doubled up the guards on our drops."

"Can't be helped, Jimmy. It is a million dollars, *hombre*. Did you ever think when we were kids we would ever see a million in cash?"

"No way."

"Me either. We are on the cusp of creating something that will sustain us past the brothels, drugs, bookmaking, and loan sharking we have always been relegated to."

"It pays the bills," Jimmy said with a stare. "It is ours and we own it. It will always be a part of our business. We can't turn it over."

"No, we can't, but we can expand, you know? We talk about this all the time. What is the cost of cleaning our money on average?"

"Forty to fifty percent."

Luis stood up quickly and started pacing behind his desk. "Fifty percent. We must work twice as hard nowadays anyway, and for fifty percent. What if we kept one hundred percent? We would double our production, and with no risk, in legitimate operations."

Jimmy could see Luis was on his soapbox again. His passion was always about diversification outside of the usual organized crime. New ways to make money. "Luis, we don't need to clean all the money. We do just fine in cash here."

"Until you need to pay rent, a car, travel, or get sick, Jimmy!"

"True."

Luis was obviously tired. Jimmy could see he was wearing the same clothes from yesterday. Jeans, shop boots, and a light blue button-down shirt with vertical yellow stripes. His black wool coat was on the back of the high-backed leather chair.

"Did you sleep last night?"

"A little on the couch."

"Go home, I'll call you with any updates."

"I'm gonna go by the families, I have some packages for them."

Jimmy looked at him. "Not alone."

"Yes, alone. This is my neighborhood. Anything happens here, you kill them all. Got me? *Comenzar una guerra.* I am not going to hide in my own house."

Luis walked over and opened his top drawer and pulled out two large envelopes full of cash. Ten thousand in each one. He set them on the desk. He grabbed his jacket and in one move slid into it. He placed the envelopes in each inner pocket and headed for the door.

Turning to Jimmy, he spoke. "Nothing is going to stop me from expanding our operations. We need that cash, *amigo*, to finish our projects and create real clean cash flow."

Jimmy stood up and walked toward his friend. "Can I come with you at least?"

"No, get started on those tasks. Also, I want to be more mobile. Get the boys to put half of the cash reserves into crypto. Send them out of state to make the transfers and give them new phones."

"Sure, what are you thinking?" asked Jimmy.

"I am worried about the FBI watching us. We would never know. If we make a move on the money, we get busted. We need to clean it. We need to move it out of state. Anything we can buy in Florida? I am thinking condos and restaurants. Run it through the Cayman accounts then move it to Switzerland and then Panama. Just like before, but in reverse."

"You got it; Armando has a restaurant deal with the owner. A fifty-fifty split. He needs capital for a renovation," said Jimmy.

"Where?"

"Miami Beach. Good cash flow."

Luis was scratching his head. "We vetted him?"

"No drugs, gambling, or other issues. He's a great cook, bad with money. When our accounting team takes over, we will increase profits by twenty percent. We also have a contract for future locations."

"How much does he need?"

"185k."

"Do it," Luis said. "I like Miami."

"How are the renovations coming on the Dallas multi-family building?"

"The contractor said it is 90% completed but wants his final check before he will finish it." Jimmy was annoyed and expressed it.

"Our guy?"

"No, civi!"

"Wait him out."

"We have time. That building is paid for," said Jimmy, now happy. "He'll come around. We owe him thirty-five thousand, and if we give it to him, we will never get the work done."

"It's fifty thousand at the end," Luis said, "or nothing."

"Did you ever think we would become project managers?"

"Not from where we started." Luis laughed. "What is our other option, sell drugs and kill each other over territory? That is the old way, and not a smart play. No one makes it out alive in the old scenario."

"'In the midst of chaos, there is also opportunity,'" Jimmy quoted. "Sun Tzu."

Luis smiled. "Yes, and 'Treat your men as you would your own beloved sons. And they will follow you into the deepest valley.'"

"Ahh, there is something calming about Sun Tzu, but why did I give you that book when you were just thirteen? Dangerous!" Jimmy said.

"Without you, I never would have understood it, old friend."

"Doubt that," Jimmy exclaimed.

"Our job is to give these guys the chance the ones before us never had. We will build a small empire. No one will know but us, and we will just simply blend into the background. As Sun Tzu says, 'Appear weak when you are strong, and strong when you are weak.'"

Jimmy stared at him and smiled his little smirk of understanding. Luis was the top of the pyramid and his was not a life of safety and security. He was a patriarch and a politician. A figurehead. His actions mattered and changed opinions.

Luis walked out of the room. Alone and unafraid. They were weakened, but he was going to appear strong for his men and his community.

Chapter 14

J en was anxious to get the kids ready for school, fed, and ready for the day. She wanted to check and make sure Cal was safe, but she had so much to do.

Equipped with a mom bathrobe, matching light blue fuzzy slippers, and a stern tone, she made her way down the wooden stairs and started flipping on the lights in the kitchen and living room.

Jen gathered book bags and shoes and set them all by the front door.

She opened the bags and then went to the refrigerator. The lunches were made last night, so she grabbed the boxes from inside and walked them over to the book bags and slid them inside. She checked and made sure all bags had water bottles and then headed back to the kitchen.

Jen turned on the stove and started gathering the ingredients for eggs and bacon. The smell would drift upstairs in a moment where the kids were getting dressed. Soon they would crash the kitchen in a desperate attempt to eat before the 7:20 am cutoff time, the time they needed to leave and head for the car.

Ben was driving them to school today. Jen was so happy to be married to such a great guy that would let her stay in her bathrobe occasionally.

She turned off the burners and set the pans with scrambled eggs and bacon on the beige tile counter tops. She did not like the look of them, but she did like the ability to set the hot pans directly on the tiles. One day, this nineties kitchen would get a much-needed upgrade. The oak wood cabinets, the tile counter tops, and terrible tile floors all needed to be rescued.

She pulled out five plates and divided the eight eggs between them. One strip of bacon for every plate except Ben's, he got three.

The youngest and most attentive to the clock came down the stairs first; Calem, who'd just turned seven years old. Next, Noel, age nine, came running after wearing only one shoe.

"Mom, I need my shoe," Noel screamed.

"By the door, honey," Jen retorted.

Noel shuffled over to the door. "Thanks!"

Calem quietly climbed onto the barstool and started devouring his eggs. He was the youngest but by far the easiest child. Good grades, homework done on time, and a great disposition.

"Good morning, Calem," Jen whispered.

"Hi, Mom," he replied

Noel came over to the counter with both shoes on and jumped into her chair. "Do we have any orange juice?" she asked.

"Of course, dear," she said and went to get her a glass.

Mike was the oldest and loudest child. He came leaping down the stairs, missing several. At thirteen, he was the most dangerous and sneaky of all her children.

"Hey, Mikey, did you finish your homework?" she asked.

"Sure, Mom."

"Is that a yes?" she asked again.

"I'll do it at school."

"Mikey, I want you to do something for me, please," Jen asked with urgency.

"What, Mom?"

"Try harder with your schoolwork," she asked pleadingly.

"Willow, hurry up, breakfast is ready," Jen yelled up the stairs. Her eleven- almost twelve-year-old daughter was probably still in the bathroom brushing her hair. "Willow!"

"She is on the way," said Ben who had snuck down the stairs and was making a direct route for the bacon. "Mmmm, bacon!"

"Oh, Dad," said Noel, "you do love bacon."

"I love my family, all of you, and of course our mascot, your Mom's bacon."

Calem started laughing. "Bacon is our mascot?"

"Of course," Ben said. "We have a family crest with two large strips of bacon crossing in the middle. A small pig is in the corner, and at the top it says Brown. To the right it has some eggs and orange juice."

Even Mikey was laughing at this commentary. Thirteen-year-olds are careful with what they laugh at, but Ben always had Mikey laughing. They both had a dry sense of humor and it was infectious.

Willow stepped off the bottom step and said, "We are not clan Bacon, we are clan Brown."

"You may not know this, but our ancestors changed it at Ellis Island," Mikey quickly retorted. "They thought we needed something more Americanized."

Everyone thought this was hilarious and started laughing and chuckling hard.

"Two minutes," Jen said.

All the family sat and focused on their food for two minutes while Jen made a tumbler of coffee with cream and two sweeteners for Ben.

"Here ya go, my love."

"Thanks so much," Ben said and gave her a kiss on the mouth.

"To the bacon wagon," Mikey screamed.

All the kids laughed and headed to the front door except for Willow. She was nibbling on some eggs and grabbed the bacon in her right hand and then headed for the door at a snail's pace.

"Do you have everything?" asked Jen.

"Nope, we usually forget something, but it will be fine," replied Ben.

"All kids get in the Suburban," she said in her best mom tone.

"Bye, Mom," came the replies.

Ben came over and planted a longer kiss on her lips.

"Love you," he whispered.

"You too."

"Check on your brother."

"I will."

The garage door closed, and silence came over the house. Jen went to the cookie jar in the kitchen and grabbed the new cell phone. She powered it on and read the message from Cal.

"Good idea," she said.

Jen proceeded to search the web for the next couple hours. She wanted to help her brother stay off the radar. She had a list of things to help him. A new low budget car or maybe an RV? She compiled a list and even reached out to a couple sellers about the condition and availability of their travel trailers. Finally, she sent Cal three options.

One in Bristol, VA. The second one was in Wytheville, VA, and the third was in Greenville, NC. All were under five thousand dollars.

She found an old F-150 with a towing hitch in Johnson City. It was brown and looked to be in good shape. The cost was thirty-five hundred. However, Cal did need an upgrade for his plan.

She typed all the information out and saved the email to the draft folder. Then deleted the old drafts.

Jen powered down the phone, returning it to the hiding place and heading upstairs to shower and get back to her normal routine. The bathrobe was not a great look after 8:00 am.

After a shower and putting on clothes, she descended the stairs and returned to the coffee maker. She made a fresh pot and waited.

She was thinking about Cal and his idea of living off the grid for a while. They all wanted to see who came looking, if anyone. It just seemed like an extreme measure to her. He would be safer with them.

The image of him in the hospital flashed in her mind. Cal told her he would never let that happen to her or Ben. He was leaving and quickly. If someone came around, call the cops. He was going to be fine. He had money and time.

Jen knew Cal's money situation. He had roughly sixty thousand in cash, three credit cards for emergencies, and in a pickle, he could always get a wire from her or Ben.

Ben was now in charge of Cal's finances. They had sat down the first night back from the hospital. Around the kitchen table, Cal wrote out on a legal pad his current financial situation.

He owned the house and his SUV. He owed about one hundred thousand on the house and about five thousand on the Jeep.

The rest of his bills were easy. Under a thousand dollars was to be paid off on his credit cards. These were work expenses primarily, and the reimbursement check was already submitted. The money would land in his account at the end of the month.

The rest of his bills were related to the house. Water, gas, electric, mobile phone, insurance payment, and garbage expenses rounded out everything. Jen had commented that his life seemed quite easy and simple to handle. Cal had agreed and then laughed.

Ben wrote down all the balances on the legal pad. In addition, he wrote down all the logins and passwords of the accounts. Together, as a safety measure, they changed all the passwords for the online payment sites.

Ben was now in charge of making sure all the payments were auto drafting correctly. Cal had called his supervisor and explained the home invasion and that he was convalescing with his family and would not be able to return to work for a while. The boss was very sympathetic and understanding. Cal told him he would check back in with him in a couple weeks, but he had no plans to return to work right away. The boss, worried now, asked him if he needed anything. Cal assured him all he need was time to heal, thanked him, and hung up the phone.

Cal then gave Ben his banking account information, and they logged into the account. In his checking account was eleven thousand dollars. His savings account had thirty-eight thousand dollars in it earning about one percent.

Ben evaluated all the bills and assumed even without any new deposits in the checking account, Cal would be fine for at least six months. "You really don't spend much money do you?" he had said.

The coffee maker beeped. Jen went to it and poured a fresh cup of coffee. Added some sweetener and a little milk from the fridge. She held the warm cup in her hand and stared out the French doors in the backyard. Leaves were covering the ground, and it had been that way for months. Lawn care was not important to her or Ben. Getting through the wear and tear of a normal school week was enough. The old days of dropping the kids off at a childcare facility was over.

Everything needed to be completed by 3:20 pm. The bus arrival time. At that time, the chaos ensued. Dinner needed to be prepped and started. Homework battle lines were drawn. Playing or fighting. Cleaning up and friends over. Crying and gnashing of teeth. This was the job. Jen had been an emergency room nurse for five years, but now she was a stay-at-home mom/boss. It was all chaos but caring for four kids was just a different form of it.

However, before the busy time of the day, Jen was enjoying her coffee in peace. This gave her a moment to plan the rest of the day and get a head start.

Ben had stayed home a couple days when Jen went to a midweek wedding in California last year. He declared he was not well-suited for the job, but insisted he was not well-suited for the after-school melee at all. He was being honest, but Jen thought he had done very well considering. Yes, he had yelled a lot more and refused to accept the "new math." He was teaching the traditional way when she got home from the airport, and the kids said it was easier. "Indeed," he said.

The important thing was he was trying and being active. He loved those kids. In bed that night, Ben expressed his devotion for Jen and recognized her for all her hard work.

They had a standing joke now. For the next twelve years their life was all about eating, getting sleep, driving the kids around, paying the bills, and somehow finding money for clothes and school programs, sports, and music lessons.

Then it was party time. Some island somewhere. Or at least a vacation now and again.

A memory sparked in her mind. Groceries. They had little in the refrigerator, and she needed to load up before the buses dropped off the kids.

She was making notes on a legal pad on the counter when the doorbell rang.

Looking over her shoulder and glancing through the glass on the sides of the door, she could see the outline of two men standing in her doorway.

She picked up her phone and called Ben.

"Hey, hon—"

"Two men at the door. Stay on the line with me."

"OK."

Jenn walked to the door slowly and looked out of the glass.

"Police officers, not Atlanta."

She opened the door a crack.

She asked, "Can I help you?"

"Yes, ma'am, I'm Officer Collins and this is Officer Denny. We are looking for Calvin Wilson."

"He's not here. I'm his sister, but he does not live here."

"Ma'am, it was our understanding that he left with you from the hospital two days ago."

"He did," she said. "He was injured in a home invasion, and we picked him up at the hospital and brought him here. He was hurt really bad, and we sent him to a recovery center out in Arizona."

She and Ben had rehearsed this story the night before.

In reality, Ben had driven Cal back to Springdale early yesterday morning. They had pulled off the side of the road before reaching Cal's house. It was around six in the morning, and the light was just starting to rise above the mountains. The glowing pink and orange haze appeared as a bright city on the other side of the mountain. In a moment it would crest the top, and the brightness would crash down across the valley and illuminate everything.

Cal moved quickly and crossed the field and entered the house through the backdoor. He walked through his house observing the differences. Jen and Ben had done a great job putting it back together again. However, it was an approximation and not how he had arranged everything. The pictures were in different places, and his items were not where he would keep them. Case in point. He was looking for his suitcase. Cal kept it in his hall closet. It was not there. He looked around, eventually finding it in his bedroom closet. He threw it on the bed and started to load it with clothes and toiletries. He zipped it closed and went next to his bed where he kept an iPad and his chargers. He also grabbed his work suitcase from beside his bed, which was already packed, and went to the kitchen. It had been tossed but it looked like everything was still inside. It was just an overnight bag, and small, too small for the all the money.

Unplugging all the equipment around the kitchen, he continued this activity around the house. He did not know how long he would be gone, so he turned the thermostat down to fifty degrees.

He grabbed both suitcases and walked out the front door. He quickly locked the house and left. He opened the back of his white Jeep and put the bags in the back. He walked down to the freshly dug grave and apologized to Daisy for not being there for her. He looked around, saw nothing, and quickly left.

Ben followed him out to the Starbucks, and they spoke for a moment while getting some fresh coffee.

"So now you will get lost for a while?" asked Ben.

"Yep, time to heal up and get out of here."

"Do you think anyone saw you?" asked Ben.

"No, my house is too hard to watch. Not too many places to observe it. Just the place you parked. Otherwise you are on the main road. We got in and out quickly."

"I need to head to work. Call me on the new cells if you need anything."

"I will, and thanks."

"No worries, stay safe, bro."

They both walked out to their vehicles with large coffees in hand. They would head in different directions. Ben heading south to Atlanta, and Cal going east into the mountains.

"Arizona you say?" asked the officer.

"Yes, he is at a recovery center. He called us when he checked in, but he can't have a cell phone there. So, we have to wait a while for the next call."

"We just need to follow up with him regarding the attack," said Officer Collins.

"If you leave me your card, I will pass it on."

"I am out of cards." Collins looked at Denny.

"I have one, here," said Denny and passed him a card from his top pocket.

"Officer Denny of the Springdale Police Department," she read aloud. "I will get him the message."

Officer Denny had turned around and took two steps down the brick porch. "How long will he be gone?" Officer Denny was asking over his shoulder.

"I don't really know. It is up to his doctors and I'm sure more likely the insurance company," Jen said smiling.

"Thanks for your time," said Officer Collins. "Please have him reach out to us when he returns. We need to get a formal statement for the file."

"Not a problem. Please find the animals who did this to him."

"We will do our best, ma'am," said Collins.

Jen closed the door as the two men slowly walked back to an unmarked black Mustang.

Chapter 15

Young Luis started reading Jimmy's books that day. He was captivated.

He started his literary journey with *The Art of War*. He found it hard at first to concentrate on the page. His mind was jumping around, and the words were written in an odd way. An old way. Soon his mind adjusted, and he was smoothly turning the pages. If he did not understand something, he went back and read it repeatedly.

His plan was to buy a dictionary. There were several pages marked with strips of ripped up paper he needed to go back to and dissect.

The words took him to Asia and beyond. He could see the battles being fought in his mind. His battle with Eddie was his background thought. What was being described had him already recalculating his own plans to beat Eddie.

He read aloud to himself. "'Let your plans be dark and impenetrable as night, and when you move, fall like a thunderbolt.'" This lesson Luis was proud of. He had told no one of his plans out of fear they would stop him, try to take over, or that he would owe someone else for his victory.

His plans were indeed only his and safe in his mind. However, those plans were changing as he continued to read. It was like caffeine for his mind, and it was awake now and working overtime.

He grabbed a pad of paper and started writing down his favorite passages. If he was to return the book, he wanted to remember some of his favorites.

Just then a noise came from down below. It was Eddie's monster. He was early. It was only noon. The day was bright and sunny, and Luis was sitting up on the corner of the roof behind some metal barrels. He had perfect line of sight to his target.

Luis decided to call him Biff. Luis hoped he was as dumb as a Biff.

He waited and saw no sign of Eddie. A few buyers came by, and Biff sold his smack, and then he did something new. He took a break and began looking around the alley on the side of the building.

Luis believed he was looking for a good hide. It took him a while, but he discovered a drainpipe not connected to the roof and pushed a bag up the pipe.

"Nice spot, Biff. Was it the drugs or the cash?"

Luis wrote it down on the pad.

Biff relieved himself in the alley and then made his way back to his spot under the awning of the abandoned hardware store. The triangular nature of the building was perfect to be able to see several streets merging at once. It gave the confidence of being able to see trouble coming, and that was why Luis had chosen it over a year ago.

Luis went back to his book. He did not think Eddie would show up for a while. Biff slowly began to grind out two more sales in the hour while Luis was learning about strategy.

Luis was tired of reading and crawled out of sight and went back to his room. There he made a sandwich and looked over his notepad.

He had learned if an opponent was stronger, then evade. Biff was stronger, but was he smarter?

Later that evening when it got dark, Eddie drove up in his IROC Z28, blue with a white racing stripe. Biff walked over to the window and a shouting match erupted.

Luis from his vantage point could hear almost every word.

"Cops shook me down, took the cash," Biff was saying.

"You idiot. You keep all the cash on you?"

"It all happened so fast. I did not have time for a drop. They must have been watching me."

"How much they get?"

"Five hundred twenty," Biff blurted.

"You moron, don't keep all the money on you," Eddie was screaming. "I can't see you every day. Find a stash and hide it until we meet. Hell, I'll go with you to get it."

"Yes, Boss," Biff whimpered.

"How's it been tonight?"

"It's good, made a hundy."

"Give me that. We will settle tomorrow. Be at my place at noon."

"Noon?"

"Yes, you damn fool, noon. We need to get you straight. Bring all the crank you have left. I'll have some H for you, just got a shipment in."

"Yeah, Boss."

"You hear anything from the locals about our guys?" Eddie asked.

"Nothing."

"I'm gonna watch from down the street for a while. You keep selling."

"Do you have any food? I'm starving!"

"Yeah."

Eddie walked to the car and handed Biff a bag of what looked like burgers. The bag was full.

"Leave me one of those, moron, they ain't all yours," Eddie chastised Biff.

"Sorry, Boss, I'm just real hungry."

"Go make me some money."

"Yeah, Boss, thanks for the grub."

Eddie didn't even acknowledge him. He slid into his ride and drove down the street about two blocks. He turned the vehicle around so he could face Biff and pulled to the side of the road in front of an old, rusty Buick. He turned off the ignition and waited.

Something came to Luis' mind. Something he had read earlier in the day.

'If your enemy is secure at all points, be prepared for him. If he is in superior strength, evade him. If your opponent is temperamental, seek to irritate him. Pretend to be weak, that he may grow arrogant. If he is taking his ease, give him no rest. If his forces are united, separate them. If sovereign and subject are in accord, put division between them. Attack him where he is unprepared, appear where you are not expected.'

Luis was thinking hard. They are already separated. Eddie is alone. He is also temperamental, so I must irritate him.

He grabbed his knife and his gun, put on a black hoodie and black pants, and finally came down off the roof. He walked two blocks down and hid around the corner till he was sure no one could see him. He crossed the street and went behind the alley and the old hardware store. He walked to his garage and went in the backdoor. The smell was starting to get bad in here. Several dead bodies in a trunk will do that.

In the back room of the shop was a large parts area. He walked over to the shelves and, with a flashlight, started looking for a box. It took him a few minutes, but he soon found it. He grabbed a handful of two-inch galvanized roofing nails and put them in his pocket.

He decided that he needed to move fast. This place was beginning to stink, and his timeframe for beating this opponent was getting shorter.

He walked four blocks on the parallel street to the one Eddie was on. He crossed over and came up behind him. Hiding behind the Buick, he could see Eddie. His driver's side window was down, and he was smoking a cigarette. A few people were hanging around Biff, and Eddie was watching closely. Luis thought he could hear some rap coming from inside the car. That should muffle his sounds. He put up his hood and sneaked around the front of the Buick and crawled under the rear bumper of the IROC. He pulled the nails from his pocket and placed a pile under each rear tire. Then he retreated to the roof.

Eddie was true to his word. After almost two hours he was bored and walked over to Biff and collected the money from the evening. Luis figured he would not let this idiot carry it off tonight.

They walked together back to the car. Biff squeezed his huge frame into the passenger side, and Eddie drove off fast. Maybe too fast for the nails to work. There was a little tire squeal and off they went. He was headed into TSG territory when he swung the car around and drifted his tail. He straightened out and headed back toward his part of town. They made it about twelve blocks. The tires were both flat. Luis could not see what was going on, but from his vantage point, he could see the headlights. The car was not moving anymore.

He laughed to himself. Irritating the enemy was fun. He left the roof and robbed Biff of his precious stolen loot hidden in the drainpipe. He also made sure to remove any of his goods from the hiding spots just in case Biff was forgetful.

He walked down the street and got about two blocks from the action. From here, he could hear Eddie shouting.

"Worst damn street ever. Why the hell did I take this shithole?"

"Money, Boss," came the reply.

"I know that."

They were not changing the tire. They were sitting on the car waiting for someone to arrive. This would put a crimp in their plans tonight and a small setback in Eddie's wallet. More important, Luis hoped it would reduce the number of visits to the area.

He walked back to the Buick. Using the flashlight, he started picking up the nails.

After a few minutes of looking, he felt he had them all. So, he went to bed. Richer and happier for causing these Titans so much irritation.

"What a good night," he said to himself.

The next morning, Luis made his way to the TSG gang head-quarters. It was not on Thirteenth Street. In fact, Thirteenth Street was actually a nice street. The name of the gang was not local. It was a chapter of gangs across the southeast.

Here they set up on the second floor of a former men's clothing store on Martin Luther King Boulevard. This was the main head-quarters of the gang. This was where all payments were collected. The bookmaking operation was located here, and on the third floor was a place for men to find companionship. Out front were always two or three members sitting at tables and watching the street. The main door was locked, and a guard had to let you in. Once in, you could roam all around the first floor. There were bunk rooms and bathrooms. Wide open areas filled with supplies. Food, beer, wine, liquor, TVs, radio, and basically anything that could go missing.

This was a collection area. If you made a bet and couldn't pay, your stuff went here. If you had no stuff to take, the gang broke something for you. Most of the time an arm or leg. If you still did not pay and the vig, or interest, was running the whole time, you went missing.

All this stuff would make its way out the back loading docks and be sold to pawn shops or right on the street to whoever wanted it. The cash was always brought back and placed in the basement safe. An old walk-in safe from the 1920s. The store had used it to keep valuable merchandise and cash in before banks were safe. Now the gang had retrofitted it and used it as theirs. They even built fake cin-der block walls and hung drywall and put rough paint on them to hide the location. A secret door led into the safe room. Large steel doors blocked the access to the large staircase upstairs. The only way down to the basement.

Luis walked past the steel doors and made his way up the stairs to have a word with Jimmy. He knocked on the door at the top of the stairs. It opened and a young initiate named Pedro opened the door for him.

"Hey, Pedro," Luis said.

"What's up, Luis? Got mountains of money to change out?"

"Naw, just a little. How you doing?"

"Good, man. Just learning the ropes here."

Pedro was older than Luis, about fourteen years old. Luis had met most of the initiates, but there were some he did not know. Pedro was a good guy and a nice one. Pedro followed up with, "How's the crew you're on?"

"Good, man, I got to go on my first big drop yesterday hauling H."

"How was that?"

"Exciting, but nothing happened. Drove to the pickup, watched Cesar do the hand-off for the stuff, and we came home. Pretty boring, but I did get a pistol."

"That's cool, you still got it?"

"Naw, Cesar took it back."

"How's being the lone ranger out there at the end of our territory?"

"Not bad."

"I heard the guys talking about you. They said that area was always fought over, and no one really keeps it for long, but you have had it with no problems for a year."

"Really?"

"Yeah, I guess a bunch of guys died there before you took over in a fight with the Blacks."

"Why the hell did I get it then?"

"I guess somebody had to," Pedro replied. "They say the Blacks want it because the neighborhood has so many working stiffs. They all work at the factories by the river. It used to be a good neighborhood back in the day."

"Yeah, Fridays are the best days," Luis admitted.

"Dumbass working stiffs. Oh, we will take their money, but don't try to get me to work in a factory all my life. They will probably die the first day of retirement. Bullshit. I'm gonna live my life."

"*Yo tambien, amigo,*" Luis replied. "I gotta see Jimmy, I'll see you later."

"*Adios.*"

Jimmy was drinking coffee and writing on his legal pad when Luis walked into the room.

"Luis, *mi amigo, aquí,*" Jimmy yelled across the room. "You want coffee?"

"Yeah," Luis yelled back.

Everyone was looking at Jimmy and Luis. This was the golden goose. No issue, no problems, he was the perfect pet. Jimmy kept him fed, and that was it. The other crew leaders were a little envious. He was also out on his own at thirteen, which was unheard of. Most guys wanted the family atmosphere of the dorms. The camaraderie. The drinking. The drugs. The fun times. Not Luis, this guy lived to work.

Jimmy poured Luis a cup of black coffee and set it next to him at the long wood table.

"Morning, Luis," he said. "Feeling better?"

"*Bien, como estas?*"

"I'm always well. Just working on an idea to make some money with a basketball game."

"You fix basketball games?"

"Not really, but an opportunity has come up," Jimmy said with a big grin on his face."

"'Opportunities multiply as they are seized,'" replied Luis.

"Alright, you've been reading Sun Tzu," Jimmy retorted. "Well done. What did you think?"

"It is really good. When you think about why the sayings are right, it takes you on a battle in your mind, and you can see the outcome."

Jimmy began quoting, "'Victorious warriors win first and then go to war, while defeated warriors go to war first and then seek to win.'"

"Explain that one to me," Luis asked.

"Well, let me put it to you in this context. We have a Tennessee game coming up verses Tech, and Tech is a huge underdog. However, what if the leading scorer, the whole reason for the ranking, were to have an injury that day? Would that type of information put me in an opportunity to win before the game even began?"

"I guess so," Luis answered.

"So, the game has not started. A point has not been scored, but I am in a position to win with this knowledge."

Luis perked up. "I get it now. So, the information gives you the advantage and a possibility of knowing the outcome before it begins."

"Yes, little man, knowledge can be more powerful than a sword, a gun, or a whole army."

"So, in this case, Tennessee is seeking to win, but Tech has already won," Luis commented.

"Yep!" Jimmy was excited that Luis understood this twenty-five-hundred-year-old ancient Chinese strategist and military leader.

"How did you manage that?" Luis asked.

"His mom is into us for a lot of cash, drug habit and betting on her son. Never would have let anyone else ride up such a tab, but I knew we could use her. Told her son I would cover her debts and find a couple thousand for him on the side. Otherwise, she may have a beating coming."

"Is it a sure thing?" asked Luis.

"No, but we are betting Tech beats the spread. We just have to keep it within eleven points," Jimmy explained.

"How much are you betting?" asked Luis.

"Everything I got. Eighteen."

"Why risk it all?" asked Luis.

"Life is a risk, little man, but sometimes you can put the odds in your favor and reduce the overall risk. That is the time to bet big. If I lose, it was a reasonable gamble. If I win, I am taking a share up the ladder and I am moving up in their eyes. Understand?"

"I do," Luis said. "Can I add to your bet?"

"How much?" asked Jimmy.

"Everything I got!"

"As long as we both are all in, then yes."

"Great, I'll be back later with the cash," Luis whispered. "I think I have about twenty-six hundred."

"How the hell?" asked Jimmy.

"I saved it."

"You always surprise me, little man," Jimmy said. "But hey, keep this quiet. If it got out, the spread would change. Tell no one."

"No problem," said Luis.

They sat in silence drinking their coffee for a while. Finally, Jimmy leaned over to him and asked, "What are you going to read next?"

"I guess *Lord of the Flies*, sounds weird."

"That is perfect for you, my rooftop friend. It's all about the perception of power and what happens when the illusion fades and the true nature of man is revealed."

"I'll start right away," Luis said. "Oh yeah, almost forgot, here is four fifty, can I get some H this time? It sells the best on my corner."

Jimmy stared at Luis for a long moment.

"Come with me," Jimmy whispered. Jimmy took him out of the main room and down the hall to a corner room. Jimmy knocked on the door.

"Yeah," came the reply.

Jimmy walked in and motioned for Luis to follow.

"Hey, Tank, got a question for you. Do we have any H available? My little man here is asking. Said there is a need on his block."

"Yeah, just got some yesterday," said Tank. "Didn't tell anyone yet. Who's the little guy asking?"

"Tank, meet Luis, my best earner," Jimmy said with pride.

"This is the kid out on Forty-Fifth and Vine?" asked Tank.

"This is him," Jimmy replied.

Tank stood up and walked over to Luis. He was indeed a tank. He was a massive human being. He stood at least six foot three or four, but it was not his height that was so impressive, it was his wide body. He was the size of at least three men.

"Nice to meet you, kid," said Tank and stuck out his hand. Luis shook his massive hand and nodded.

"How did you know about the H, kid?" asked Tank.

"Word got around," Luis responded.

"I bet it did. This stuff is so hard to get right now. Our connections got busted at the border several times, and we are stuck with nothing but the dirty cut crank we have."

"How much did we get?" asked Jimmy.

"Twice the normal load, but it will go fast. I want twice as much for this load, we are behind," replied Tank.

"Not going to be a problem, it's dry out there," said Luis.

"Good, you can have a taste of it, kid. More next time, OK?"

"Yes, sir," Luis replied. He was a little bit intimidated by the size of the man, and the sir just popped out.

"Sir, I like that. Call me sir, Jimmy," Tank said while pointing a massive finger at Jimmy.

"Yes, sir," replied Jimmy.

"Get out of here. Go see Jose and tell him to give the kid five hundred bucks' worth, but remember that is half the normal. I bet you can mark it up even more, though."

"Thank you," replied Luis.

They went down to the basement and gathered the bag, half of it empty and the little foils of heroine falling all over the table.

Luis dropped five hundred on the table, and he and Jimmy climbed the stairs.

"So, do you want twenty-one hundred on Tech still?" asked Jimmy.

"No, I still have the twenty-six hundred. This is work money," came the reply.

Jimmy smiled and thought how he had won the lottery with this kid.

"Bring it to me today. I need to make a bet by six tonight."

Later, Luis returned and brought Jimmy all his cash in a potato chip bag and asked him if he wanted the rest of his chips. Jimmy looked inside and smiled.

Chapter 16

Sitting on the rooftop, young Luis determined his plans needed to be accelerated. The bodies in the garage needed to be moved and soon. The problem with Crazy Eddie also needed to conclude before the end of the week. Today was Tuesday.

Luis was convinced by Jimmy those warriors and strategists in history eventually had to attack. Irritation and deception could only be used for so long before a battle must be started.

The Titans had been a troublesome neighbor for too long, and Luis wanted to put a buffer zone between his corner and the Titan controlled territories. Or, if he could, he would try to take all their territory.

Luis went to the HQ to recruit some help. He spoke to his other low-level wannabes. He explained how they could gain some street cred and they would get a share of whatever was captured. Six agreed to follow Luis.

Only four showed up on his Luis' rooftop the next afternoon. Pedro, Juan, Ricardo, and Jose showed up packing. They each had a weapon of some kind. Luis was impressed.

"Any problems getting the guns?" Luis asked.

"Naw, no big deal," Pedro responded.

Jose picked up his plaid shirt to reveal a Glock 26 with a clip that held nine rounds.

"Woah, where did you get that?" asked Luis who was holding his little rusty thirty-eight. "Glocks are badass."

"Got if off Bullseye. He won't miss it. It was hidden in his room with a bunch of others," came the reply.

"You stole from Bullseye?" asked Pedro.

"Let's just do this, and I may put it back," Jose said with a lot of attitude.

These guys all knew what was at stake. To become a member, you had to prove yourself. You needed to make money, be a good soldier, and stand out at the same time. Getting a chance to stand out was a hard road. Waiting for something to happen or an opportunity to arise to prove yourself could take a lifetime, so you had to make it happen. Luis had provided the opportunity, and these four were going to take it.

Luis went over the plan with them. He had already posted a note for Biff down below. In a little while, Eddie would show up with his men at the garage. They would look in the trunk. Who could resist the smell coming out of there? He would see his guys. They would retreat out of there to regroup and think.

Luis' crew would follow them to their headquarters, observe their strength, and take a risk.

Pedro and Jose went in search of a car.

"Why don't we just hit them at the garage?" asked Pedro.

Jose, who was looking down the street for any vehicle, responded, "Luis understands that this will not end by hitting Crazy Eddie. The Titans will just send the next wannabes or initiates into his area. Then a member or crew leader."

"So why follow them to their HQ?" asked Pedro.

"It really is the only choice. We need to take out everyone from here to their HQ, and then we clean them out. Money, guns, drugs, and those streets. We will own it all. No more begging for scraps. We will be balling in it."

Pedro liked this prospect. "I like it."

Jose continued. "It will also take out a large number of them, and they will be weak. Then we take a piece to Bullseye and tell him to hit them hard everywhere else."

Pedro was getting it now. He started smiling. "So, we are the heroes, and we get our own area?" he asked.

"Now you got it."

Luis and Ricardo were on the roof watching for Biff to arrive. Ricardo was looking around at the barrels that were set up and the watcher stands Luis had built.

"How long you been up here?" asked Ricardo. He was an incredibly quiet kid, but when he spoke, you could tell he had thought about it and worked it out in his mind before the words ever hit his lips.

"Three weeks," said Luis. "Maybe more."

"You must like the rooftop. I don't like heights."

"Yeah, it is away from everyone, and I can see people coming," replied Luis.

"Well, Rooftop, I hope this works," said Ricardo.

"Rooftop?"

"Yeah, it suits you," Ricardo said.

The two didn't speak much till the others returned. Luis thought how great it was not to have to fill the time with talking. He was starting to like Ricardo.

Pedro and Jose climbed the stairs and jumped on the roof.

"Anyone show up?" Pedro asked.

"Not yet, you find some wheels?" asked Ricardo.

"We got one, it's a slow and ugly Ford Tempo."

"Perfect," said Luis. "We need to blend in."

"Time to get ready," Luis said. "Load your guns and get your masks ready. It's getting dark."

At that, Jose's stomach started a large growl. Ricardo smiled and Pedro laughed. "Hey, I'm starving," said Jose.

"Probably nerves," said Ricardo.

"Naw, I'm really hungry."

"Let's eat," said Luis. "I got some sandwiches and cokes for while we wait."

"Nice," said Jose.

Thirty-seven minutes later, Biff showed up in a Ford pickup truck.

"That him?" asked Jose.

"Yup."

Biff walked over to the front of the store to his leaning post. He noticed the fliers Luis had pasted on the post and the front of the store.

He read it.

"Crazy Eddie, we are ready to make a deal. If you want to know about your missing guys, meet me at midnight in the garage two blocks behind you."

They all watched as Biff took out his phone and made a call.

"Eddie, there is a note here for you." He read it to Eddie. "OK, Boss, I'll see you then."

"Now we wait," said Luis.

Three hours later, Crazy Eddie slowed his car down in front of the hardware store and Biff got in. Three other cars were following him. They turned at the corner and made their way to the garage.

"Let's go," said Luis.

The crew ran to the waiting Ford Tempo and drove about five blocks from their location and parked on the side of the road.

Ten minutes later, four cars came speeding by them and headed into Titan territory. Pedro started the car with no lights on and followed behind the last car. At several points they got too far ahead, but Pedro caught back up to keep them in sight.

There were a lot of directions being given to Pedro from every seat except Ricardo's.

"Guys, I got it. Settle down," said Pedro.

Pedro continued to follow at a distance of about twenty car lengths. Then the lead car's headlights turned left at the light.

"Left coming," said Luis.

"See it."

When the last car turned left, Pedro turned on the lights. They were on side streets now and they did not want to look like a drive-by was about to happen.

They noticed they were far behind now, but luckily, they were turning into an old restaurant.

"See that?" asked Pedro.

"Yeah, park here," said Luis.

They all waited in the car as they watched about fifteen people walk in the restaurant.

"More than I thought," said Jose.

"They were expecting something, and they were ready for it," said Luis. "Here, they feel safe. We will wait twenty minutes and then go."

The team went in and attacked the room with bravery and a lack of fear only present in the hardest of soldiers. They entered and began firing. This was the signal, and Ricardo with a shotgun came in the backdoor with Juan and his machine gun. The two of them were dropping those scrambling for the exits. Ricardo picked up fallen weapons and continued fighting when he ran out of shells.

Turned out there were over twenty men in the restaurant. Eddie had called in the bosses, and they were waiting for them with their captains. They were sitting down to discuss what had occurred when the little crew burst in the door.

The rest of the men were getting high in the corner or watching television. All were caught off guard.

Gunfire was only one-sided at first coming from the front door. The men at the table were falling in rapid succession. Moments later, rapid fire and large booms came from the back.

The two teams converged into the main hall where the crossfire was deadly, only pausing for a moment to reload or pick up dropped weapons and start firing.

It was the perfect example of bravery and stupidity. If you were to plan it out, this would never work. But the fact was, all the little crew needed was the will to win and the determination to keep going. They never blinked, hesitated, or stopped moving further into the restaurant. This was deadly, especially to the ill prepared.

The Titans finally started returning fire, but it was too late. They were cornered in the back by a large stone fireplace and a mass of overturned old wood tables and chairs. They were returning fire, but the four just kneeled, got low, and started firing. The four teenagers, now all with automatic weapons picked up off the ground, unloaded hundreds of rounds into the tables. The result was devastating. No one was left. Eleven men fell to the ground.

The damage was minimal to the little crew. Pedro was hit in the arm, but it was only a graze. Luis had broken glass cuts across his face from some glasses they shattered with return fire. Jose stood without a scratch on him, Glock in his belt and machine gun in his hand. Juan was covered in blood. Apparently, as everyone learned later, Juan and Ricardo busted in the back door with Juan leading because of the machine gun. When he ran into the first Titans heading for the exit, he opened fire. Immediately, several men fell. One, however, taking several bullets to the chest, rushed Juan and got all the way to him. He began choking Juan until Ricardo cracked his skull with the butt of the sawed-off shotgun. Blood covered Juan's face and chest. His throat hurt, but he was fine. Ricardo, using his four shells rapidly and effectively, dropped the shotgun and picked up a handgun and MAC-10. A ricochet hit him in the thigh but barely penetrated the skin. He picked it out later with a knife.

This story was to be told over and over again not only by TSG but by all the gangs around. Five kids took on twenty Titans in their own HQ and took them all down.

When it was done. Luis gave a lot of credit to Jose, calling him Glock from that day forward. He had ten shots in his gun, and as Luis told it, he dropped all ten men he aimed at.

The five of them were alive, but they did not slow down. They started moving quickly through the restaurant. They searched everyone. Taking money, jewelry, wallets, drugs, and all the weapons in the room, they headed for the trunk of the car.

They had made three trips each back to the car which Pedro had brought up to the backdoor. The trunk was emptied and filled with guns, then bags of loot, and then finally, Luis found a false wall that had been damaged by a shotgun blast. On the other side was a manager's office. He went in and pulled the wall away. Inside he found a full string light. It illuminated the tiny nook. He could see ledgers, money, and documents. They grabbed it all. Ten minutes later, with police sirens blaring, the response time was obviously lacking in this part of town, they made their way back to the garage where they unloaded their loot in the supply room, and Pedro drove off the old car to dispose of the bodies.

This fused the little crew together for a lifetime. There was nothing one of them would not do for another. It also made them and gave them a brutal reputation. They were feared. Now, they were also rich. Rich in information, cash, guns, ammo, and drugs. The information was the more important thing. The ledgers were worth the whole raid. Luis and Ricardo poured over the ledgers, putting together the whole business of the Titans and how they made money. They assumed ownership of all the loan sharking, gambling debts, and the drug trade on the previously owned Titan streets.

They collected easily. Their methods had been laid out. People feared the name Rooftop and the Little TSG.

Soon Jimmy and Bullseye would pay them a visit to find out what had been happening, but more importantly, to get a taste of the action. Only the Little TSGs knew what the total take was, but they gave Jimmy five thousand dollars. To Bullseye, they gave an M16 because they knew he would appreciate it, and they had six more. He was happy with the gun, but when they handed him a bag with fifteen thousand dollars inside, he could not believe it.

"They had this much cash on hand?" he asked.

"We sold the jewelry and took cash off everyone," replied Luis. "We got about fifty thousand total, including product to sell. Is thirty percent not enough? We thought that was the right number to bump up to you, considering."

Luis knew it was really only fifteen to twenty percent depending on the score, but he was making a statement. Leave us alone and we will produce for you.

"Little man, I accept your generous gift," Bullseye said. "What do you need from the TSG?"

Luis thought about it. "We want to become full members and the territory we just took to be ours from my old corner to the downtown."

"Ballsy, aren't you?" Bullseye said. "Can you hold it?"

"We took out all senior leadership and almost every captain we knew about," Ricardo said.

He threw all the IDs on the table in front of them. There were nineteen driver's licenses sitting on the table, most of them from older and more senior leaders.

Bullseye recognized some of them right away.

"You will need help," Bullseye commented. "It's a big area and no offense to you five, but because of your age, you will not be taken as seriously, AS YOU SHOULD BE!"

Jimmy stepped up to the table. "I'm in," he said. "I have nothing but respect for Luis and everything he has ever done."

"It's Rooftop now," retorted Ricardo.

"Suits you, Rooftop," said Jimmy.

"It does, don't it?" Bullseye commented. "He is your initiate; you should be here with him."

"Not anymore," said Jimmy.

"Agreed."

Juan stepped up and announced, "As long as everyone understands who is in charge here. It's not me, or Pedro, Jose, or Ricardo. We work for Rooftop. Jimmy, that means you too."

Bullseye looked at him with a disapproving smirk. "You OK with that?" he asked.

"He would be in charge no matter if I was the face man or not," Jimmy said. "Let's make it clear from the start, so I don't get stabbed in the back later."

They all laughed at this but knew it was true. One day the thirteen-year-old would be a man, and he would not take orders from Jimmy anymore. Best to do away with the illusions and let him lead.

Chapter 17

His wounds and his nervousness prevented Cal from immediate sleep. The uncomfortable rawness of a short back seat added to the discomfort. The bruised body was healing but was still tight and sore. All these things combined to create an inability to get comfortable.

Cal had been driving through the mountains and spending time sightseeing. No real place to go. No itinerary. Getting lost.

His main goal was to create some distance between himself and the rest of his family. He did not want them to be involved, and he believed this would help to prevent their involvement.

After a full day of driving in the Appalachian Mountains of Georgia and North Carolina, Cal found himself on the interstate at ten o'clock at night. He was tired and wanted to formulate a better plan. He had just passed Asheville, NC, and was still heading north on I-26. He had been looking for a rest area to stop and look at his new phone. As he was heading up a long steep hill, he saw a sign for a scenic overlook. He made his way off the exit and found one of the eight parking spaces and pulled in. There was a family with four dogs all walking in the grass next to their truck and travel trailer.

That was a great idea, a small travel trailer with a bed and a little kitchen. He could be off the grid and live easily. His cash would last him longer, and he could still be mobile.

He focused back on the issue at hand. He had no idea where he would stay that night and had a limited understanding of hotel policies for cash. Who used cash for hotels? You'd miss the points.

Tonight's problem was not getting fixed. He opened his phone and started looking for hotels. There were a couple independent hotels about twenty-five miles up the road in Erwin. Bed bugs did not sound like a great start to the trip. Cal did not like independent hotels after a bad experience. He was at a sold-out conference and the only availability was at a small independent hotel about ten miles away. He checked in at the lobby with the smell of curry and lots of Indian decorations lining the lobby walls.

His problem came when he checked in and found the corner of the bed moving with small brown bugs. He went back to the desk and he got another room.

The new room was not a lot better in the cleanliness factor, but at least he could not spot any bugs. He searched all around and found trash behind the bed and a used condom behind the nightstand but no bugs. He left his bags on the tile floor in the bathroom hoping they would stay safe there.

He climbed into bed after eleven o'clock at night, exhausted from traveling all day. He woke up at 2:00 am with his face itching. He went to the bathroom to find splotches on his face and arms. It looked like some reaction to something. He washed and washed his face. He took a shower. Put his underwear in the trash. Changed his clothes and went out and slept in the car. It took two days for the splotches to go down. It was not a great trip.

"No more cheap hotels," he said out loud.

He grabbed his wool coat, turned off the engine, and climbed into the back seat.

After about ten minutes of laying on his side, he started to drift away, but he always caught himself. His nerves were shot, and he was worried about the police coming by and tapping on the window, or some crazy person looking for teens making out but settling for him. He ended up staring into the night until the pain of sleepiness took over. He had a hard time lifting his head. Cal gave in and drifted away.

He awoke later to the sound of an eighteen-wheeler pulling in the outlook and parking perpendicular to the parking spots off the main drive. He pulled himself up by holding onto the headrest. He could see the cab of the truck directly behind him. The driver was crawling back into the cab and the lights went off. "I feel the same, brother."

If he is not a serial killer, it will be nice to have someone else here on this mountain's edge, he thought. Cal laid back down and shifted to his side with the coat rolled up in a ball under his head. His jacket had shifted when he got up and had fallen under the door handle and was not comfortable. Cal moved it around to a good spot and was soon asleep.

At 3:00 am he woke up with the sound of the eighteen-wheeler's engine starting up. He noticed for the first time he was cold. He had been sleeping on top of the sleeping bag for comfort. He thought it near impossible to climb into the bag in the tight confines of the back seat. The softness of the bag had made the difficulties of sleeping across the back seats and seat belts bearable.

Another feeling was stronger than that of the cold. His bladder was full, to the extent of not being able to fall back asleep. He contemplated this for a moment as he knew he would have to get out of the vehicle to relieve himself.

Nope, it was inevitable, he had to go.

Cal pulled himself upright out of his side position in the back seat. He sat there for a moment and looked around. His feet were not touching the floorboard because of the supplies of food and water sitting there.

No one else was awake. "This sucks," he said to himself. His earlier idea of just staying in the car and being mobile was now a discredited idea.

He was over six feet tall; this was not a long-term solution to hiding out.

He was thinking about all the cabins and campgrounds he had seen on his drive. They take cash, right? I will do some research and find something better.

He reached across the front seats and unlocked the doors on the driver's side. He was afraid to unlock the car from the back seat and possibly set off the car alarm. He heard the loud click as all the door locks sprung free at once.

He reached up and unhooked the tag from clothes hook by the oh shit handle. What the hell is this hook called? We know what an oh shit handle is. Universal, he thought. It's probably called oh shit in every country. No one knows what the clothes hook for dry cleaning is called. Maybe just clothes hook? Boring, he thought.

He took the shirt down and lifted the headrest which held the arm of the shirt tight and in place. It had stretched out the shirt but had been necessary to block out the light from the streetlamp in the parking lot. It had a direct line of sight to his face when he was lying flat in the backseat. It had been very annoying at the beginning of the night, and his makeshift solution had worked well.

He lifted the door handle and slid out into to cool early morning. Had to be in the low thirties, he thought. The morning air was wet and fresh.

His body was upright for the first time in a while, and he took the time to stretch it out.

He slowly began walking forward.

The streetlight had illuminated the whole area and there was a good place right in front of the car.

He continued to walk forward, up and over the curb, and down the sloping grass field. The night air was so amazing.

He felt like a kid again. What adult would be up at 3:00 am unless coming home drunk? Then the idea of the night air and peacefulness of the mountains would probably be lost.

His mind was running wild with ideas, and he felt more and more awake. His mind was active now, and he thought he might not get back to sleep.

An RV or trailer, yes, that was the best option. Tow your hideout with you. He liked the freedom and opportunity it presented.

Down the slope about twenty feet and towards a tree, he kept walking. He turned and could see the top of the cab of the eighteen-wheeler. So, he kept walking about fifteen more feet downhill. He turned again and saw the green/gray bank of the hill.

This was his spot.

He stood in the middle of a sloping field, looking out at the interstate below as it climbed up the hill. The interstate was deserted, and he did not see any lights.

He stared at the quiet trees and shadows until the pain reminded him of why he was out here in the first place. He unzipped his pants and started to relieve himself. The only sound he heard was the hot urine as it hit cold leaves and ground.

His head rolled back and that was when he saw it. Stars. Numerous stars everywhere. Even with the streetlight up on the hill, he could see thousands of stars. The sky was ablaze with them. He was entranced and excited to try and find the constellations he knew. Immediately, he found Orion's belt and traced out the hunter with his mind.

Up to the left, he saw Gemini, the twins. He could easily find this one. It looked like two stick figures laying down and holding hands.

To the right of Orion, he saw Taurus. However, he could still never understand why that was a bull. He knew the two branching horns were horns. The rest of it was a bit much to imagine.

Nature had been calling to him. He felt like he was finally awake in his body. Something about being awake at 3:00 am on a cold mountaintop was special to him. It was a small awakening in his mind and body. The beauty of the night sky had captivated him. He was attempting to commit it all to memory. This was something he did not want to forget.

Driving through the mountains that day had been great, and was inspiring to a small degree, but this was something different. Something more intimate with nature.

He was opening up inside to something new and exciting, and this was a first step. A first step to what, he had no idea. He liked it just the same. He finished his activity, and the chill of the air was starting to get to him.

He stood there anyway, defiant against the cold. A jacket would have been a good idea, he thought. Time to go back to the car.

He slowly walked back to the car. He was looking for the stars as he made his way under the streetlight. He could see a couple bright stars, but the ethereal beauty was gone.

He climbed into the driver's side and started the car. He turned up the heater to full.

Previously tired, now he was awake. If he had been at home, he would be sleeping comfortably on a bed, but he would have missed out on what he just experienced. The survival instinct he was running on was coming to the surface. He looked around and made sure he did not see anything.

Reaching into the center console, he took out his new cell phone and turned it on. It took a minute, but once it was powered up, he checked his email and messages.

Nothing new.

He typed out a short email to Jen and Ben, letting them know he was safe. Saving it as a draft, he closed out his email program. They would check the account every day and see it in the folder. Open it and read the draft. This way no messages were being sent.

Jen had thought of this after hearing a tale from one of her girlfriends at her divorce party. Apparently, the wife had been having a very long-term affair in which no one knew about. After the divorce was final, the girlfriends became privy to the information, after four or five long island iced teas.

To communicate with her lover, she explained they used this technique to exchange information and meetup times. When it was passed to the other person, they deleted the draft and emptied the trash. No record. Jen would do the same thing for their messages.

Maybe he was being too paranoid. However, there was a lot of money at stake. Money that people would kill for. He was still sore, and the images of the beating popped into his head. He had suffered enough already. He needed to keep himself and his family safe.

He wanted Jen to have full deniability, and no electronic records would ruin it. Clean and simple.

At the end of the normal email, Cal had added something new. He told Jen that sleeping in the car was horrible and could she please find him a tiny travel trailer? Basically, a bed and kitchen. He guessed they might cost less than five thousand dollars but would be well worth it, and to search in North Carolina or southern Virginia so he could drive to it. He ended the message with: Love, Cal.

He was now warm and ready to go back to sleep. He put the phone to sleep and placed it back in the center console.

Then he turned off the engine and climbed through to the back seat.

This time he managed to wiggle his feet into the bottom of the sleeping bag and unzip it to make a large blanket that he pulled over top of him. He moved to his side with his back to the seats, curled up in the fetal position.

The next time he woke up, it was to sunlight. The sun was coming up over the mountains and illuminating the ground on the hill and the slope of the previous night. Color was coming back into his vision.

He was tired of sleeping and wanted some coffee. Not hopeful of a good coffee shop in the middle of nowhere, he turned his attention to a diner or waffle house.

Rising slowly, his breath was visible in the car. The windows were fogged up, and it appeared as if frost was on the hood of the car.

Time for a repeat performance. He walked back to his same spot and again did his business. Getting back into the car, he left the scenic overlook and made his way north.

The heater was on, and the car seemed charged and ready for a full day of activity. His stomach growled its first growl of the day.

"I've got to get it together. This is miserable. I'm rich, after all."

Chapter 18

The meeting between the Russian representative and the TSG was scheduled for 5:00 pm in the old national cemetery. The Russians had pushed for a meeting on neutral ground, but Luis had said no, it would be in Knoxville.

The Russians had made some bad decisions recently. To brush off the notorious Rooftop would be the worst one yet. He was smart and ruthless. More importantly, he was somehow connected to the Mexican cartel. The Russians sent their number two guy to meet with him.

The coffee shop was warm, and the front windows were covered in a hazy steam making it hard to see out. Nikolai was sitting at a table in the back. This was one of the old-style coffee shops of the nineteen fifties. The ones where you'd get coffee, a waitress, and a breakfast. Called, The Coffee House, it was about five blocks from the cemetery.

Nikolai was an important man in the Russian organization. He was the face man and second-in-command. He lived in New Jersey and had flown down for this meeting.

He oversaw a distribution system from New York to Florida. Although he often worked with local organizations, he was not part of a gang. His men were spread too thin with only small cells in each city they did business in.

He did not want to have this meeting, but his boss, the man behind the curtain, wanted this fixed. There was too much money on the line. If the cartel and the gangs shut them out, there would be hell to pay.

Nikolai had brought crews from four surrounding cities into Knoxville. The head of his crews was walking in the door now. He was glancing up at the clock over the counter, four o'clock. He spotted Nikolai and made his way through the aisle toward the back of the restaurant.

Viktor took his gloves off as he greeted his boss.

"Good evening, Boss," he said respectfully in a heavy Russian accent.

"Are we set up?" asked Nikolai.

"We are," he replied.

He slid out of his jacket and sat down in the wood booth.

"Coffee?"

"Please," responded Viktor.

Nikolai looked at the young woman who had served him. "Miss, a cup of coffee, please."

"Coming right up," she replied.

Viktor studied his boss, the man he spoke to on the phone regularly but rarely saw in person.

Nikolai was about forty-five years old with slight gray streaks in his full but trimmed goatee. Jet black hair. An olive complexion with a strong but long nose. Not a face you would forget. His eyes seemed not to fit his face. They were light brown with almost a green tint. They were narrow and appeared to be hiding something.

Nothing else was out of place with him. He wore a nice dark gray wool suit with a jet-black cashmere knee length overcoat. His black leather gloves sat on the table.

"What have you found out?" asked Nikolai.

"Word on the street is Rooftop lost the money in the shootout, thinks we boosted it from him. He is wanting restitution."

"Not going to happen," said Nikolai. "The trade was clean."

"Yes, but our guys went to boost it on the way home."

"That is not the problem of the organization. Is it?" asked Nikolai with alarming intensity.

"No, sir, but it was our men and everyone knows it. They were lying dead at the scene with his men."

"What does he want?" asked Nikolai.

"He wants the money; he is sure one of our men took it."

"None of our men made it out alive," spat Nikolai as he spoke.

"I guess he does not know that," Viktor reported. "Rooftop is blaming us for the death of his men and the loss of the money from the exchange. He will want his money back and restitution for his loss of life. Which is not out of line. After all, they did try to rip him off."

"I am not authorized to give him all of that." Nikolai looked sternly at Viktor. "You will be by my side and will say nothing, understand?"

"Yes, Boss," Viktor responded.

The coffee arrived and more cream and sugar was placed in the middle of the wood table.

Viktor slowly sipped his coffee in silence. He was thinking about what would go down in an hour. He had placed four crews in and around the cemetery. Two with black Suburbans, automatic weapons, and body armor. One unseen. He had them set up on the hilltop a hundred yards away. They had sniper rifles and plenty of ammunition.

This was not a typical meeting, and Viktor was not taking any chances. If he was going to be put in the middle of the action, he would take precautions.

Viktor let out a sigh. He did not like this operation. First, he did not like being up front in the kill zone. He was a soldier. He wanted to be armed and conducting security, but Nikolai was in charge. He would make sure his men did not have itchy trigger fingers.

His jacket pocket buzzed. He reached in and pulled out a radio. He hooked up his earpiece, placed the earbud in his left ear, and placed the radio back in his jacket pocket.

He heard his men checking in. Each of the three teams checked in and had nothing new to report.

Viktor went back to his coffee.

When the time came to make their way to the cemetery, Viktor had finished four cups of coffee. He took a bathroom break and then put on his coat and stood by Nikolai as they made their way down the street.

Checking in for the last time with his teams, Viktor announced, "Be sharp, everyone. It's time, don't get me shot."

Nikolai and Viktor were waiting for Luis and Jimmy for about five minutes when they observed Luis' SUVs pulling up along the narrow, winding blacktop road.

The four men met in the middle of the cemetery surrounded by headstones and the occasional crypt. An open but not public venue. Each had two vehicles with men stationed at each. Part of the agreement was only two cars. Jimmy had handled the negotiations and made sure all was adhered to.

"Glad you showed up, but I had asked for your boss," stated Luis.

"I am Nikolai…"

"I know who you are and him too, but I wanted to speak to Vitali, your boss," said Luis.

"He does not take these meetings; it is below his station."

"How about I fly to Toronto to see him, can you make that happen?" asked Luis.

Nikolai thought about it. "What if you just went away? We can make that happen."

Luis laughed, but Jimmy was rigid. Luis was off script. Jimmy was searching for the reason.

Luis replied, "I think you have me confused with a common gangster only interested in the little things."

"What do you mean?" asked Nikolai.

"I mean, I need my money back, but not for booze and partying." Luis was pacing and talking. "Not for women and drugs. We have those things already. I need the money for expansion."

"Expansion?" asked Nikolai. "Where?"

"Well, we have chapters across the south, but I have bigger plans. Plans of a larger pyramid where we are at the top."

"Where?" Nikolai asked again.

"Toronto," replied Luis.

"Impossible! We are in Toronto," said Nikolai. He was outraged now. What was happening here? Nikolai was a smart man, and he did not see any reason why he would announce this information to anyone, unless this was a shakedown to stay out of his territory, which was seven hundred miles away. Toronto was wide open, with the Canadian government and the police forces being decades behind the United States in organized crime policing. Plus, they had no RICO Act, the Racketeer Influenced and Corrupt Organizations Act. They were setting up gang task forces in some cities, but as a country, it was wide open for organized crime, and they wanted a monopoly.

"You see, when I wanted a word with you," said Luis pointing at Nikolai, "I put it out there to our chapters in other cities. I went through my contacts in Washington, D.C., Atlanta, and Miami. We threatened to cut you out of the trade. No guns, drugs, or young Mexican girls you love so much."

"I am aware."

"What you are not aware of is that I own those chapters," said Luis. "You see, I have been providing them with drugs and guns for almost fifteen years, and they report to me and pay me a large percentage to protect them and guide them. I bought the Thirteenth Street name with blood and made it my own. Now, if you want in, you pay me every month."

"So, you are a little bigger than we thought," said Nikolai. "Why are you telling me this?"

"Simple, your people stole from me. Killed four of my guys and then you refused to have a sit-down with me until I involved your bread-and-butter business in Miami, Washington, D.C., and Atlanta."

"We were trying to find out what happened," exclaimed Nikolai.

"I am sure you were," said Luis. "More like, where is your cut?"

"No, we did not get the cash. In fact, no one got the cash. All four guys who went after your crew died. My men have confirmed it. We investigated them and it checks out. The rest of our crews are clean and were accounted for. We did our homework."

"I see," said Luis. He looked over at Jimmy, and Jimmy shrugged his shoulders. "So, what you're telling me is your guys chased my guys. Got into a gun battle. All died. No money. That is what you're telling me?"

"Yes, we checked it out. The four who went after you were not sanctioned. They figured they would hit a small-town gang but got in over their heads at the marina. No one made it out alive."

"Off book?" asked Luis. "They were not acting on your behalf is what you're saying."

"That is correct, we did not sanction it, and did not even know about it."

"When did your guys split up?"

"After the exchange. Our runners took the merchandise to Charlotte and met our trucks. The other crew must have left then. Turned on their jammers and followed your crew back here."

"But they did not end up here."

"No," said Nikolai. "Looks like they deviated from the plan and ended up in Springdale."

Luis turned his back to Nikolai and walked over to Jimmy. Jimmy was standing very still and straight as a board. Luis leaned in, whispering.

"What do you think?" asked Luis.

"This guy just gave you license to kill them all. You know it's not his guys who have the money. They did too much searching for it, internally. Not for us, but for themselves, they would have found it. That leaves the Feds or local cops in Springdale. Feds would have bragged. Taken pictures with it. Nope, it's the local yokels."

"It is indeed," replied Luis. "Anything else we need from this guy?"

"I'd like to know where our dope is right now," replied Jimmy.

"Not me, most of it is baking soda."

"Luis, what the fuck?" asked Jimmy. "So, you wanted this meeting, even if the money was not stolen? Why?"

"To take our next step forward, to colder climates."

"You wanted these guys here. Did you ask for Nikolai?" asked Jimmy.

"No, I wanted the boss, not his number two, but it is all good. My new crew in Toronto is going to bust down their compound in five minutes and get the boss. Besides, the boss is an ex-KGB figurehead. This is the man behind the curtain. He runs the whole show."

"I better not get shot," Jimmy whispered.

Luis cracked a big smile and suppressed a laugh. "You have that Glock still, right?" asked Luis.

"Yeah…"

Luis turned and walked back toward Nikolai. Viktor stepped one step toward Luis. Luis saw this move as an attempt to intimidate him. He put his hand up toward Viktor's chest.

"Calm down," Luis said. "My man and I discussed it. You owe us compensation for our men we lost. Four of them. How do you plan to make it right?"

Nikolai stepped forward with confidence. He thought he had made progress now that the two million was off the table. "What type of compensation?"

"I would think some of our dope returned to us. Give us six kilos back."

Nikolai was hesitant to answer. Obviously, something had gone very wrong on the exchange in North Carolina. He had the drugs, but four of his men were dead in some small town in Tennessee and four of the TSG were dead as well. Nikolai was not consulted on this, but if it had worked, he knew he would have a nice cut. It failed and men were dead. Some type of reparations would have to be paid. Six kilos was not out of the realm of possibility, but he needed that for the shipment to England. He had the twenty-six plus kilos now in Atlanta. It would soon be on a private plane to Canada and then broken up and some sent to England.

He did not want to give up any of that shipment. It was worth over one hundred and fifty thousand a kilo in Canada or England.

"Six is high," Nikolai complained.

"It's not," said Luis. "Bring me the six kilos so I can pay the families."

"We don't have it here."

"Why not, you knew you would need something to compensate us. What did you bring?"

Nikolai motioned to Viktor. Viktor nodded and slowly took his walkie out of his pocket.

"Bring the case," Viktor barked into the radio.

There was movement around the Suburbans, and a man in black body armor walked a case up the hill and toward the meeting. He handed the case to Viktor and returned to his position. Viktor opened the case and showed Luis.

"There is two hundred and fifty thousand," Nikolai said proudly.

"I would rather have my kees back."

"Sorry, that delivery is about to be shipped out of the country," Nikolai said. "This is the best option right now."

"You can have it back here in a day," Luis was taunting him. "The coast is not that far."

"We are not using the boats anymore, too risky. We need to fly it out of the country," Nikolai said.

"Well, bring me the six and you keep the rest."

"No, I'm sorry," said Nikolai. He was tired of this. He was making a generous offer and was getting frustrated. "I am not able to adjust the shipment. It is already packed into the plane. It took our guys three days to tear it apart and rebuild it."

"OK."

Jimmy walked forward and took the case. He closed it and let it hang by his side.

"We good?" asked Nikolai.

Luis gave the thumbs-up and held it into the air. Two seconds later, Viktor and Nikolai's heads exploded, and they fell back on the cold, wet ground.

Luis dove on top of Jimmy, pulling him to the ground.

"This way," Luis yelled. They crawled around monuments in the direction of their vehicles as gunfire erupted from the hilltop and the Russians at the SUVs.

Gunfire poured down from the hilltop pinning them down, and the men in body armor came charging toward Jimmy and Luis. Luis grabbed Jimmy and pulled him behind a large monument. Shots rang out from the Suburbans. Bullets began hitting the monument. Jimmy and Luis got as low as possible.

Crews were moving up from behind them with bulletproof vests and machine guns.

Jimmy yelled, "They have body armor."

Luis handed Jimmy his radio.

Jimmy yelled into the radio, "They have body armor, aim for the head."

From the hilltop, a piercing shot rang out, and the Russian front man fell backward a few feet and crashed into the ground after being hit in the chest.

The crew leader, Pedro, made his way to Luis and was putting a flack vest on him.

"What the hell was that?" asked Jimmy.

"They had a sniper crew up there with some huge guns. Sounds like the boys are having fun with them," said Pedro.

"Get Jimmy a vest," ordered Luis.

"It's coming," said Pedro.

Two of Pedro's guys were making their way around monuments on their way to Luis and Jimmy.

Pedro started firing at the oncoming attackers. He kept a steady stream of fire to allow his men to reach his position. The attackers were moving up slowly and had reached the first man on the ground. Pedro stood up and shot a rapid succession of bullets at the man on the ground and the legs of the attackers. One man fell next to the first man who was hit again.

A few seconds later, a steady torrent of gunfire erupted about twenty feet to the left of Jimmy.

"Whoa, on our left." Jimmy tapped the man on the shoulder handing him a vest. "Over there."

The two men moved toward a monument on the left and began shooting.

At that moment, two shots rang out in succession from the hill. The men on the left where hit in the back. Thinking they were covered from above, they charged out into the open when the TSG men, using their newly obtained sniper rifles, put them down. The men on Jimmy's left moved forward and fired several shots into the men who were lying face down on the ground.

There were three men left in the middle, but they were dragging a wounded man back toward the Suburbans.

Jimmy yelled into the radio, "Close in. They are headed for the cars."

Luis grabbed the radio. "Shoot the engine block with that cannon up there." Luis was laughing now. A moment later, the hood popped up on the first Suburban and the second one followed a moment later. Steam and smoke were pouring out of the front of the vehicles.

"Damn."

Pedro yelled to his men. "Let's go."

The three of them moved quickly across the open area of headstones and stayed low. The other crew was coming up from the road on the other side of the Suburban. Three men in body armor were making their way up the hill. They realized they could not make it any further across the flat field of monuments.

More shots rang out as all three points fired at once. From the road, the middle, and the hill.

All three men fell.

Pedro ran forward and shot all three in the head.

"Check those cars," Pedro yelled. "Then head out, grab all the weapons."

His men were already on the field picking up guns.

Jimmy walked over and searched Nikolai and Viktor. He took their phones, handguns, a notepad, and some strong looking cigarettes.

Jimmy's voice came across the radio. "*Adios*, boys."

Chapter 19

Luis glanced up from the table, looked around. His eyes settled on a modern art looking clock behind the counter. "Jose says they usually come in at their shift changes. One around 6:00 am and again around 2:00 pm."

"Free coffee?" asked Jimmy.

"Of course. These guys own this small town."

"They certainly make more money than any small-town cops anywhere in America," stated Luis.

Luis and Jimmy found the fancy little coffee shop in Springdale entertaining. Sipping expensive lattes and munching on gluten-free muffins, these hardened men sat and observed the middle-class soccer moms and their habits.

"Maybe we should get a female crew out here. Dress them up in yoga pants and two-hundred-dollar sneakers."

"What would they sell, oxi?" asked Jimmy.

"Among other things. I bet the weed market alone is worth four or five hundred grand here."

"I'm sure it is, but these people need edibles, not smokes."

"Agreed, let's make muffins and gummies with weak doses," said Luis. "They will love it."

"I'll talk to our cut shop when I get back, has to be someone who can bake something in there." Jimmy was laughing to himself. This type of world was foreign to him but at the same time fake. A house of cards, debt, and student loans. He saw all this as stressful as his life. "They are probably tired of cutting coke with baking soda all day anyway. Who wouldn't want a little baking to ease the stress?"

"If they build it and it works, it could be its own crew with royalties. Sell it in every market from here to Miami."

"We have the stuff but working in this white lady area is gonna be tough," stated Jimmy.

"I know, but I can dream," said Luis. "One day our weed business will dry up when it all becomes legal."

"We need to have this kind of new income. Plus, I really like yoga pants."

They both laughed loudly and caught themselves.

Luis stood up and went to the counter to get a refill.

When he returned, he noticed Jimmy watching the door.

"These are our guys."

Two officers in blue walked in the door. One was a tall and beefy with broad shoulders and a thick neck. The other was average height, weight, and plain-faced with sunglasses on.

"Their shift is over now," said Jimmy. "They come here before heading home. They sit in the corner and, who knows, catch up at the end of the day. They are in separate cars but basically partners."

"Time to go."

Jimmy and Luis had not only had all the cops followed, but a small dossier was opened on all twelve Springdale Police Department officers.

Not much information was coming out of it. Social media gave a lot of information, but none of it revealed who might have the money.

Luis started contacting his people who could speak to the Mayor of Springdale, Mayor King. They knew he had nefarious dealings with some of the same people the gang used. In addition, they found out through sources he was tied to some shady land deals, extortion, and bribery. This was a man they could talk to. They opened the communication pipeline.

Jimmy reached out to the mayor through his money launderer named Fitzgerald. Fitz had worked for both parties at different times, and he agreed, for a small fee, to introduce Jimmy to the mayor. He arranged for the two men to meet at a downtown hotel bar in Knoxville.

Fitz had assured Mayor King it was a legitimate meeting and in his best interest to attend. King was wary of the meeting, knowing what he knew about the attempted robbery of the gang's men, but he went anyway. If he refused, it might draw attention to him, and this was not something he was willing to do. This was an opportunity to learn what they knew and how much.

They sat together at a corner booth near the entrance to the hotel. It was a busy time, and no one paid them any attention. They both ordered bourbon on the rocks and waited to speak until their drinks had arrived.

Jimmy explained the need to find and deal with some people who had stolen money from his organization.

The mayor was understanding and engaging. His willingness to help caught Jimmy off guard. Or was it just the politician in him seeing an angle?

He did not offer Jimmy any information but was happy to listen to his problems.

Jimmy decided to try a new tactic. He offered the mayor a reward for any information on the stolen cash. Two hundred and fifty thousand dollars in cash.

The mayor was seventy-five percent sure the boys had not found the money. He knew they beat the hell out of a suspect on Windy Hill Road, but nothing had come from it. Or had it? Would they be hiding the money from him?

Jimmy and the mayor exchanged email information. Jimmy told him to only email "yes" if he had information, and they would meet here the next evening at 7:00 pm.

Mayor King agreed.

Three days later, Mayor King sent the email.

Jimmy and the mayor met again. This time Jimmy brought the case of money from the cemetery. He showed Mayor King the cash. The mayor, who had obviously been thinking about how to play this out, was more subdued than before.

"I want to be completely anonymous in this," stated the mayor.

"Of course, Mayor," Jimmy replied. "We want to find our missing money, nothing more. In addition, we will owe you a favor. It is a good place to be in. If you have issues in the future, you come to me. We will fix it. If you need help moving something or cleaning it, you come to me. Also, if someone tries to shake you down or intimidate you, I am your first call, I'll take care of it.

"I can offer you one more thing," Jimmy added.

"What is that?"

"We will open up this area for small high-end operations including marijuana and designer drugs and pills," said Jimmy with a smug look. "You will earn ten percent of the operations."

"Gangs in our town, no, I don't think that will work," retorted the mayor.

"Not gangs, white kids, selling to white ladies, a whole network of people who will blend in and stay under the radar."

"Interesting." The mayor, who was still on the fence, was now feeling the love and his own importance. He also liked the idea of a favor. The mayor did understand what this meant. He would have protection from the gang, and that was better than any amount of money. Mayor King now felt taller, stronger, and even a little invincible. He had made his decision.

"The men you are looking for are two police officers at Springdale PD," whispered King.

"Names?" asked Jimmy. He slid the case from his right side to his left and next to the mayor.

"Collins and Denny," replied the mayor.

"They have the money?" asked Jimmy.

"I don't know if they do or do not," retorted the mayor. "I know they were out on that Friday night in an unmarked car and did not check in once. The car came back missing a lot of fuel and had a large amount of mileage."

"Do you think their names are worth a quarter million cash?" asked Jimmy. "Because I don't. I need real intel."

"This is the type of thing they are into."

"Again, I need something real."

"Look, they came to me after the fact and told me about the money. They said it was out there and they had followed the cars from the casino. They said there was a shootout at the marina."

"They were at the marina?" asked Jimmy.

"They arrived about thirty seconds behind the last car, and it was over by then."

"So, did they find any money?" asked Jimmy. Jimmy was tired of pulling the information from Mayor King, but he knew this path was guiding him to more and more information, and maybe the mayor might slip up from his story. Jimmy was not buying the mayor's version. He knew way too much.

"No money, but they did have a look around."

"No, money?" asked Jimmy.

"So they tell me. They said they retraced the route and looked for it but never found anything. Said they even questioned homeowners on the road. One guy, they put in the hospital late one night when they came back to search his house. They did not like his answers, and it was a part of the road where they had a blind spot on the chase."

"Do you think they are just telling you a story to cut you out?" asked Jimmy.

"No, I don't think so."

"Did they keep looking or what?" asked Jimmy.

"I don't know exactly."

"Tell me about my guy who gave him the information," said Jimmy. He was intensely eyeballing the mayor now.

"Look, I am not involved in this," croaked the mayor.

"Mayor King, we will protect you, and you will be compensated tonight with this case. Tell me about the Thirteenth Street guy."

"His name was Juan or Julio, I think. Collins interrogated him and shot him on a farm road. He gave up the deal. He wanted to avoid all the open warrants he had," said Mayor King.

"Julio?" asked Jimmy.

"Yes!"

Jimmy took a moment. He was considering all he had heard.

"OK, here is the case. Contact me if you need anything. You can always go through Fitz if it is urgent, he can find me."

"That's it?" asked the mayor.

"That's it. Keep quiet, not a word to anyone. Goodbye, Mayor."

With that, Jimmy stood and left. The mayor gulped the rest of his drink and raised his hand to the waitress. He needed at least two more.

Jimmy walked outside and called Luis.

"Got it," Jimmy said. "Heading to the shop."

"Meet you there," came the reply.

Now, two days later they sat in the parking lot of a fancy coffee shop in Springdale. Waiting for two crooked cops to emerge.

They had a plan, but cops were not going to be that easy to grab. Luckily for them, the mayor informed Jimmy of a meeting between himself, Collins, and Denny which was scheduled for tonight.

The trap was set. They would grab them leaving their farms before they ever made it into town.

"Do we have everything set up?" asked Luis.

"We are good," came the reply from the passenger seat. Jimmy never drove anywhere. He was always driven, or he rode with a crew, but never alone. Luis, on the other hand, loved to drive. He had several classic cars in storage units and would take them out from time to time.

"Just waiting for seven o'clock. The boys will gear up around 6:30 pm on their roads."

"Good."

"What do we do till then?" asked Luis.

"Let's explore this town."

"Good idea, Jimmy. We have a full tank of gas and a full cup of coffee."

They drove around town, stopping to shop and even having dinner at the local main street diner.

At 6:30 pm, Jimmy received a text from both teams. They were primed and ready for the grab.

The teams had positioned a van and a car about a half mile from each cop's house. The van appeared to have collided with the car and were half sticking out into the road.

When the cops pulled up on the scene, they got out to investigate and were met with a sliding door opening and three men with automatic weapons.

They were hog-tied, blindfolded, and their mouths taped shut. In addition, they had been searched multiple times. A gang member took their car, and everyone had headed for this rendezvous point. All in all, the event took less than two minutes.

Jimmy was exceptionally good at this. His planning and eye for detail had really sold the event. He even used smoke bombs under the hoods for dramatic effect.

Luis was ready for bloodshed, but it had gone smoothly. At the first sign of weapons, Collins and Denny had turned over their guns. On a further search, Denny had a backup on his ankle. Collins had nothing.

An hour and a half later, Collins, Denny, and Jimmy were sitting across from each other at a metal table. Jimmy was still drinking coffee, but the cops' hands and feet were zip-tied together. They were back home in an abandoned building in East Knoxville. There were at least ten gang members in the room. These guys were going nowhere.

Luis walked into the room.

"*Buenas noches, puerco!*"

Jimmy laughed, as did the whole gang. They had captured two police officers from a neighboring city and dragged them here to be interrogated. Not an easy thing to do, but it had gone to plan.

"So, these are the brave men of the Springdale PD?" asked Luis. He was playing to his audience. He wanted to make a show of this. They had killed Julio, one of their own, in cold blood. They were going to pay for that. They had gone after the gang's money, and they were going to pay for that too.

First, Luis wanted the whole story. He walked over and sat in a chair across from them. "Let me introduce myself, I'm Rooftop, head of the Thirteenth Street Gang. Thirteens, Thirteeners, or TSG."

Collins and Denny, who had been really calm until this point, stared wildly at Luis. Their eyes were large and concerned. They knew they were in trouble. If someone was so brazen as to go after a cop, they would have no trouble torturing or killing those same cops.

"Priest, files please," asked Luis.

Priest walked over with two large files on both Collins and Denny. He set them on the table in front of Luis.

"You see, we have done our research on both of you. However, we will not be playing soldier's dilemma, or first to answer, or any other torture games to extract the information I want from you."

Luis smiled real big, and for affect, he said, "Jimmy, tell them why."

Jimmy stood up. "You killed one of our own, so you are going to die. You were going to attack our crews, so you're going to die. The question is how, and will we bring your wives and children into this."

Jimmy paused. He could see the eyes of both men tearing up, and they both started fighting the restraints.

"Hold them down," Luis said.

Four men stood over them and pushed their shoulders down into their chairs.

"Now, this is going to be a civil and straightforward discussion," Luis continued. "If you hold back, and we know a great deal already, you will incur my wrath on your families."

Jimmy opened the files and pulled out Facebook pictures of the children and set them on the table facing the police officers.

Luis began, "I have no sympathy for you or for what you have done to your families. You are not saints; you are gangsters with badges."

The wiggling started up again, but the men held them in place.

Jimmy placed his phone on speaker and placed it on the table and called his crew outside of Collins' farm.

"Hey, it's me, tell me what you see."

"I see a red barn with a green tractor inside. There are some horses in the field, a white house with green shutters. A minivan with license plate TN 543-432."

At this, Collins lost it and rage took over. He pushed up hard and broke free of the men holding him. One of the gang threw an elbow, and Collins collapsed back into the chair.

A similar call was repeated at Denny's house. Denny listened intently.

Luis spoke, "So, you see, I am very serious about finding out everything you know about my missing money."

"Are you ready to answer some questions?" asked Jimmy. "Oh, and before you try it. No platitudes about how we are going to pay, or you'll never get away with this, and you will lose something important to you. Understand?"

Both men were still.

"Understand?"

They both nodded in agreement.

"Well, I guess we are ready," Jimmy stated. "Boss, they are all yours."

Luis leaned back in the chair and stared at his prey. "Tell me everything," he said.

Chapter 20

Collins and Denny had finally calmed down. They resigned themselves to the fact they would die in this room. They were going to do everything they could to protect their families.

"Tell us how you got involved," said Luis.

Collins started and explained how he had pulled over Julio Martinez on the backroad. After threatening him with life in prison, Julio had offered some information for his freedom.

"That piece of shit," said Priest.

Collins stuttered a bit and then finished the story.

He explained where Julio was buried and how they had sold the car to a fence in Atlanta. Denny jumped in and told the rest of the story of climbing into the TSG storage unit and inspecting the product.

Once they verified the story was real, they prepared for the exchange at the casino.

The plan was to follow the crew back from the casino. About five miles from the last Springdale exit, they would pass the lead vehicle and gain some distance on the crew. They would place some tack strips in a dark area on the road before the turnoff, forcing them to the exit. Here they had placed a truck and flatbed trailer waiting to move across the exit, blocking it and trapping the oncoming vehicle. They would stand behind the flatbed and hit the oncoming vehicle with automatic rifle fire. The engine block and the driver were the first targets and then shoot the entire inside of the truck before anyone could get out.

It was a solid plan, and Jimmy looked impressed. Slowing the vehicle down and hitting it hard in a quick fashion would've worked. This limited their casualties, gave them a quick exit back on the highway, and prevented anyone the opportunity to fight back. They did not need the crew alive. All they needed were the bags.

Jimmy looked at Luis, and Luis looked back. The look said it all. It would have worked. Luis was taking mental notes on how to hit a moving transfer for the future.

"What changed the plan?" asked Jimmy.

"Your crew did," said Collins. "The Russians had moved past us and got behind the TSG truck. They were not subtle about their intentions and got spotted. The truck increased speed for a half mile, and so did the Russians. Then they slowed down to the speed limit for a mile, the Russians matched them. At that moment, it was out of control. The first exit was approaching quickly, and at the last second, the lead vehicle darted off the exit and headed off through Springdale at a high rate of speed."

"The Russians' plan was busted at that point, and so was ours," said Denny. "So, we followed, hoping to find an opportunity."

"Then the chase down the road to the marina?" asked Luis.

"Yeah, and that is where the Russians opened fire," said Collins. "They were aiming for the tires, and they hit them, which is incredibly hard to do on that road."

Denny took over. "They made it to a turnout road by the marina and decided to make a stand. When the trail car turned in, they opened fire. We were about a hundred yards behind but could see it all happening. Both vehicles emptied and the shooting was loud and intense. The automatic weapons fire on both sides had everyone down within thirty seconds. We eased into the drive and saw no one standing. We took our time and approached slowly. We thought it was clear, so we searched both vehicles and all around the area. We found nothing, so we went back to clear the flatbed and then inform the mayor.

"After briefing the mayor, we all went searching for the bags, but never found anything."

"Tell us about the mayor and his role in this," said Luis.

"He's the boss," said Collins. "He gets a cut of everything we bring in, and he protects us with judges and lawyers." They further explained the mayor and his role as a small-town player with the keys to the city.

They told Luis about searching the roads for the bags, the interviews with homeowners after the sun came up, and about Calvin Wilson. They searched his place, interrogated him, and beat him to within an inch of his life, and he told them nothing. He was their best suspect, but they had nothing on him. They tore his house apart and found nothing. They did not know where the money was. His computer had revealed a search history about the shootout at the marina, and he had been researching money laundering.

Luis looked at them quietly the whole time and gave Jimmy a look. Jimmy received it and sat down across from the men. Priest moved in behind Jimmy.

"Tell me more about the mayor," asked Jimmy.

"What do you want to know?" asked Collins.

"Does he have the money?" asked Jimmy.

"How?" asked Denny.

"Did he go searching on Saturday morning?" asked Jimmy.

Denny looked up and said, "He did go out Saturday morning. After we met at his place early and explained what happened."

"Where were you two?" asked Jimmy.

"We worked backward from the marina," said Denny.

Collins added, "And the mayor went to the highway and searched through the town, I think."

Luis rolled his eyes at Jimmy. "Your mayor, he might have it. After all, he did put us on you two."

Collins' eyes burned with fire and rage. "What?" he asked.

"Oh yeah, he told us all about you two," said Jimmy. "Pretty smart really. Moves the attention off himself, onto you two."

"If he did have the money, and you two are out there trying to beat it out of people, word is going to spread," said Jimmy. "Better to just end this quietly."

"You did hit Julio, so he knows you are not getting out of here alive, and the truth will die with you," Luis added. "He probably never thought we would actually get anything out of them.

"Priest, Pedro, let's talk," said Luis.

Pedro, Luis, Jimmy, and Priest went to the corner of the building. They spoke softly and were digesting the new information.

"I spoke with the mayor and he is shifty," said Jimmy. "We should probably close that link anyway."

"Give up the mayor as a resource?" asked Pedro.

"There will be another; besides, that little white-bread town can't really offer us anything," said Luis.

"Priest, what do you think?" asked Luis.

"We kill these two and we hit that mayor. No ties to us. But first we get him to give us what he has. If he has the money, we get that. If he has other shit. We get that too. I think we will find that Mayor has the cash somewhere."

"Get my quarter million back too," said Jimmy. "I've got to put a new roof on the apartments in Miami, storm damage."

"Jesus, Jimmy, you thinking about that shit right now?" asked Pedro.

"Always, *amigo*, I got my own list of problems to solve," said Jimmy. "We are really close to having lots of positive cash flow with no risk."

"Priest is right," said Luis. "Do it. See what you find, but make it look like an accident or suicide."

"You got it, Boss," said Pedro. "I'll get Glock, we'll handle it."

"Me too," said Priest.

All of them looked at Priest. This was new. Priest had not gone hunting since he returned from prison.

"I'll make sure he talks," said Priest.

"Always welcome, *mi amigo*," said Pedro. "Let's go find us a mayor to kill."

Chapter 21

It was late when the knock came on Mayor King's door. The mayor was having a drink and watching a home renovation show.

He got up from the couch and walked the hardwood floors of his oversized mansion nestled in the fancy side of town.

He cracked the door, and Priest shoved a Glock in his face.

"Open the door," Priest said quietly.

The mayor stepped backward slowly as the three men entered his house.

"We need a quiet place to talk," said Priest. "We don't want to wake the family."

The bulky Mexican was covered in tattoos and was an intimidating figure even without the gun.

"The garage," King said, stuttering over his words.

They walked down the hall and through the kitchen to an outside door. Following the mayor, and with a gun to his head, they escorted him into his man cave, the garage.

"Nice," said Pedro. "Is that a Porsche 911?"

"Ya, yeah it is."

"Mayor, have a seat, we have some things to discuss," said Pedro.

Priest walked him over to the couch in the man cave and sat next to him. Pedro and Glock stood over him.

"First, let's start with the introductions," said Pedro. "We are TSG, and you are going to give us our money back."

"Oh God, sure, no problem, it's over there under the sink," said King.

Glock walked over to the sink and opened the cabinet door. Sitting on the floor of the cabinet was a briefcase. Glock grabbed it and set in on the counter. He opened it.

"It's all there," said King. "I have not taken anything out."

Glock said, "About 250, I guess."

"You would know," said Priest.

"Mayor, thank you for that, but I am talking about our two plus million," said Pedro.

"What are you talking about? I never got any of that money. Talk to your boss, I gave him the names of the guys responsible."

"You did, but since they are no longer with us, and they worked for you," said Priest, "that makes you responsible."

"What, are you kidding me?" said King.

"This is very simple," said Pedro. "You owe us money. If we don't get it, we will start hurting you, and then your family in front of you, understand?"

"Wait, wait, wait, I am on your side here. I am trying to help you."

Priest dug his pistol into the mayor's side.

"Last chance," said Pedro. "We don't like long interrogations. Glock, go get the wife. Call the boys to pick up the kid at the university. Tennessee, right? Good school."

The mayor burst out into tears.

"No, stop, I'll get you money. I don't have your money, but I can get you what you need," he said. "It's over there."

The mayor pointed to the workshop in the corner of the garage where a tool rack and toolboxes were built into something Martha Stewart may have designed. It looked expensive and never used. It did, however, go with the decor of the garage and man cave.

"Let's go," said Priest.

They stood up and followed the mayor to the tool benches. He reached underneath a cabinet and pushed a button. The built-in countertop and storage cabinets in front, bright yellow in color and matching the Porsche 911, moved slowly to the left, exposing a doorway. The mayor walked up and entered a code on the door panel. The door opened.

"That's far enough," said Priest. "Hold him here."

Priest entered and Glock and Pedro held the mayor in place, Glock holding him by the neck and Pedro with a gun in his back.

Priest felt around the side and found a light switch. He flipped it up. The light illuminated the small room. It was a poured concrete bunker, like a safe room or a storm shelter. In it were shelves and gun cabinets. A large safe was on the far wall next to shelves containing artworks in vacuum sealed bags.

"What's all this?" asked Glock. "Your stash house?"

"It's in the safe," said King.

"Go open it," said Glock.

"Glock, I need your eyes," said Priest.

Glock was great at buying, trading, and selling anything of value in exchange for cash or instead of moving cash. He had once accepted, instead of cash, a block of concert tickets for Metallica. It worked out well; they got the cash from the sales, plus he got to go.

"I see it," Glock responded.

One section of shelves contained sports collectibles, form cards to signed balls and bats. Another had art. Statues and busts in what looked like marble.

"Where did you get all this shit?" asked Pedro.

"I took it in exchange for deal approvals or as a percentage on the back-end," said King. "It took me a while to find a guy who could clean my cash, so I took whatever I could."

"Are those watches?" Glock asked. He moved over to a cabinet with black felt lined drawers with clear tops. Inside, he could see at least a hundred watches. From a few Rolex, Patek Philippe, Audemars Piguet, Tag Heuer, and Bell and Ross watches. This was an incredible collection, and easy to transport and easier to sell. Plus, guaranteed these were not hot. These were not million-dollar watches, but between ten thousand and forty thousand each. At least originally. These high-end watches tended to hold their value, and these still had all the boxes and paperwork in the drawer below. Glock was salivating over this. He was holding a case with a quarter million in it, and this room must hold more than a million that he could see.

Mayor King walked to the safe and placed his thumb on the scanner and entered a combination of at least eight digits. It cracked open.

"Back up now," yelled Priest. He was not going to take any chances King had a weapon in there. They needed to make this look like an accident, so roughing him up was out of the question. Shooting him would also look bad.

King complied and slowly backed up. Pedro held him in place.

Inside the safe, Priest could see gold coins, some jewelry, and thumb drives.

Glock walked over and looked. "Bitcoin?" he asked the mayor.

"Yes," said Mayor King. "I bought it when I learned how anonymous and easy it was. When I first got started with it, it was a hundred a coin, and have been using it ever since. I started taking payment in it. Easy to buy and even easier to hand someone a thumb drive. All you need is the drive. Plug it in and it is yours."

"Encrypted drive?" asked Glock.

"Nope, it is wide open currency, even passwords can incriminate you," said King.

"How much is on each?" asked Glock.

"There should be a small sticker with a number of coins on each side," King said.

Glock turned the three drives over and saw the numbers 1, 2, and 5 bitcoins written on tape and wrapped around the outside.

"That is not enough at current prices to cover your debt," said Glock. "You are way off."

"The gold is worth a lot."

"About a hundred grand, still not enough," said Glock. "Do you think we don't understand the value of this stuff?"

Pedro was searching the drawers when he found it.

"Glock, look at this." The mayor stumbled backwards, and Priest caught him.

Pedro was trying to remove a false bottom to a large bottom drawer.

Glock came over to look.

"Hold this." Pedro handed Glock his gun.

With both hands, Pedro found the seam and the tab to the cover and lifted it up. The baseball cards on top spilled onto the floor. Underneath was cash, and a lot of it.

"Looks like we have a winner here," said Pedro. "Find some rope."

It took them an hour, but they emptied the safe room and loaded the Suburban waiting outside. Pedro wanted to take the Porsche, but Priest said it needed to look legitimate. They wiped down the vault and the door handles, returned the vault to a hidden room, and walked out the door with the light on.

Chapter 22

C al found himself standing in a rural fast-food burger restaurant bathroom somewhere in the mountains of Eastern Kentucky and hoping he was not drawing too much attention with his blood-soaked flannel shirt and jeans.

Cal had made his way into the bathroom by moving quickly through the side door of the fast-food restaurant.

He was exhausted. He had been up for over twenty-four hours. He had taken a short nap on the way here when he could not keep his eyes open any longer. The lack of sleep and stress was showing in his eyes. They looked hollow and his eyes had dark circles around them, with some slight puffiness below his lower eyelids.

Cal set his backpack on the sink. The motion was slow and deliberate. He did not want to aggravate his wound. He stared into the mirror at his white and black flannel button down which was now coated in dried blood. The left top of his jeans was also covered in dried blood from the pocket down to his thigh. The blood had turned a glossy reddish-brown in color.

Lifting his shirt, he found the source of the blood. A long, superficial gash across his left rib below the breast. The pain was diminishing, and it was just sensitive to touch, but the wound looked like it should hurt more.

The knife had only grazed his side but had created a dramatic display of blood and bloodletting reminiscent of a character in a cheesy haunted house attraction. He needed to avoid people and assess the damage.

He was muttering and grunting to himself in disgust. "What were you thinking, Cal?" He had just missed being shot too, but it was the diving out of the way and landing on the parking garage floor that had scraped up his hands and arms. He rinsed the wounds and patted them dry. Cal was more disgusted with his carelessness and not the injuries he was cleaning.

Cal stared into the mirror, searching for a calm to come over him.

So much for my criminal instincts, he thought to himself. What was I thinking, buying a new ID off someone I was just introduced to? Of course they were going to rob me.

Cal was talking to the bartender the night before and a conversation came up about people escaping their lives. Cal mentioned he would like to escape his.

"How do you do that?" Cal asked

"New identification, new place, new home."

"It's that easy?" Cal questioned.

"It could be."

As it turned out, this bartender knew a guy who could get you out of the country for ten thousand dollars. Canada or the Islands. Mexico and Central America would cost more. Cal was intrigued. He wanted to have a conversation with this guy. It could be useful for the future.

"You have to have two grand just to meet this guy," said the bartender.

"So, you need to have two grand to meet him, plus ten grand to get you out of the country?" asked Cal. "This is adding up."

"Can't put a price on freedom," came the reply.

Something was off about this guy, but Cal let it go. He assumed there was a cut in it for every refugee he brought to this smuggler.

"What's his name?" asked Cal.

"They call him Blythe. Not his real name of course."

The bartender called Blythe and they arranged a meeting for six in the morning in the parking garage, top floor.

Cal brought the two thousand in casino chips. Blythe brought a knife. He wanted more, and when Cal resisted, Blythe swung at him with some kind of blade. Cal barely managed to move out of the way with the knife just grazing his ribs.

Cal did not stay to fight. He fled for the staircase. He saw a gun being pulled by Blythe's bodyguard, and he dove behind a car as the shot rang out. He did not lay there but instead took off for the stairs.

The sound of the gunshot discouraged the chase, and they ran away and did not follow. Besides, they had his two grand, a success for them.

Cal was bleeding into his flannel shirt, and he could feel the warm, wet patch on his side. He kept descending the gray concrete staircase until he reached a metal door with a red level two on the sign. He dashed to where he had left his Jeep and took off. A car came down from above and seemed to be following him.

He tore out of the parking garage and onto the street. He made quick turns and got on random roads. He headed north and kept heading north the whole way. Until he reached this bathroom.

The knife wound had ceased bleeding and had created a temporary but effective crust. The wound needed to be cleaned and might need stitches.

Cal unbuttoned the flannel shirt and took it off. He walked over to the sink and pushed the shirt down into the bottom of the trash can next to him then covered it with paper towels. He splashed some water on his face and looked at himself in the mirror. His mind was racing, but he needed to calm down and adjust to this situation.

Forty-one and still got my hair, he thought.

He was proud to still have his hair, especially with his family tree. Hairstyles were a quick and easy way to change your appearance when you were on the run, but he was just proud of his hair.

His hair was light brown. The length was professional, sides cut short, and some length on top. He had considered dyeing it to a black or even a blond, but he liked it too much to mess with it. He did not even know if he was being chased or if he needed to change his appearance. A wig was much easier, he thought.

Nothing more could be done in this bathroom, and he needed to move on.

He needed some ibuprofen or a couple shots of whiskey, but what he needed most was a bed.

Grabbing a tee shirt and hoodie from his backpack, he got dressed.

He splashed some water on his face again and adjusted his hair.

Time to invoke rule number four, see food, buy food. This was the newest rule Cal had developed. He had lost weight over the last several weeks. Almost ten pounds. The stress of hiding out. The attack. The hospital. He was not eating enough.

He headed out of the bathroom and made his way into line to place an order.

In front of him stood a girl in her mid-twenties with tattoos on her arms and a mouth that maybe had half of the teeth in working order. The other half were missing or blackened.

"What can I get ya?" she said in her mountain drawl.

"Give me a burger meal, a large water no ice, and a large Diet Coke," he said with a smile.

"You got it, hun," said the girl. "$6.82. Sorry, gotta charge ya twenty-five cents for the water, new rule."

"No problem," he said, and handed her a twenty.

She made change and handed him two large cups. He wandered over to the fountain drink machine and filled his cups, one with Diet Coke and the other with water, and waited by the counter for his order. His order number was thirty-three. He stared at the receipt until a large woman appeared.

"Thirty-three," the large woman said.

"That's me," he said. He grabbed the bag of food and turned toward the door.

Just then a deputy pulled into the parking lot. He pointed his bright white police cruiser at the windows of the restaurant.

Instead of heading for the door and risking the deputy seeing the blood on his pants, or just getting harassed for not being local, he slid into a booth on the opposite side of the restaurant from the cruiser. The restaurant was less than half full now, and a row of tables full of people blocked his view of the police officer.

He pulled a sandwich out of the bag and pretended to settle in to eat. He did not unwrap the burger but placed it on the table next to both of his drinks.

He looked at his watch. Almost eleven o'clock. He had been driving for nearly five hours. He'd stopped for a thirty-minute nap at a rest area on the Tennessee and Kentucky state line.

He looked around the place. White wall paint and red and gray booths lined the sides. White tables with metal chairs filled the middle of the restaurant in neat rows. This place was exceptionally clean, and Cal assumed they had just finished cleaning before the lunch rush. They even had two self-ordering kiosks near the entrance, but nobody was using them, and the line for the counter was now two deep on each side.

He eventually took a glance at the television mounted high up in the corner playing CNN. A news story was flashing across the bottom of the screen. Two Springdale, Tennessee, police officers had been found murdered in Atlanta.

The broadcaster was muted but explaining the situation through the closed captioning. They were found in a safe house used by some Russian crime syndicate. There was currently a huge crackdown underway from New Jersey to Miami. Arrests were made and over thirty were in custody.

The documents collected at the scene of the Springdale officers' murders pointed to a vast network of drug distribution, gun running, money laundering, human trafficking, and prostitution. There were other charges pending, but these were the top ones. The question the experts were pondering was why the organization had been so careless in leaving all this incriminating information at the scene of a brutal murder. This was the current topic of debate. Also, a large estate in Toronto had been attacked around the same time. The supposed head of the Russian organized crime syndicate was found dead. Others, a man named Nikolai Kolesov and Viktor Voronin were found dead in Tennessee. Their bodies were discovered with nine others in a Knoxville cemetery. They were wanted in their native Russia for murder, bribery, and counterfeiting. In the US, they were on a federal organized crime watch list, but no indictments had ever been filed.

The authorities explained there was a massive shootout at this cemetery, and apparently the Russians had ended up losing the engagement. Men were found on a hilltop overlooking the cemetery, near the vehicles which were shot up and inoperable, and in the middle of the graveyard. Shell casings were everywhere, but not one weapon was found on site.

New information coming in last night, the Mayor of Springdale was found dead in his garage after an apparent suicide. He had hung himself in front of his prized possession, a yellow Porsche 911. He was the Mayor of Springdale, where the two officers killed in Atlanta were from.

Cal was transfixed on the television.

"Oh, my God," he mumbled.

This was bad. There was a war zone near his home. Two local Springdale cops were dead, found in Atlanta. Meaning they were probably the ones who attacked him and were in on it from the beginning. The mayor was dead; he was probably involved.

The money was still missing, and now the Russians had been wiped out. TSG was making a huge move. They were the only ones left from the original shootout at the marina.

Atlanta, he thought. I need to talk to Jennifer.

The deputy came in and stood in line which was now three deep. He started a conversation with others in the line, so Cal gathered his things and headed to the door. He pushed through it and felt the cold breeze of the mountains in winter.

He climbed into the Jeep and started to look around.

To get here, Cal had been using the interstates, backroads, and even a logging trail to get away and was lost, driving for about three hours in no direction in the mountains. This was the first little town he had come across in a while.

He had sent his boss an email about being sick this week. Then he powered down his cell phone and tossed it under the front seat of the Jeep. He was in no hurry to replace it, time to get lost. In the mountains of Eastern Kentucky, lost was easy.

This little town seemed old, real old, and quite wild. These small towns with no connected roads to major cities tended to have a very strange aura about them. The view was beautiful, and the streets were quaint and rustic, but they also had an abandoned feel to them. In this small mountain town, there were only three commercial buildings in front of him, a burger restaurant, a dollar store, and a gas station. Down the road he could see houses on both sides of this main street as well as a ridiculously small brown brick municipal building.

This was Appalachia, small and large hills were rising all around him like a packing crate. This was a great place to get lost, but a meddlesome local sheriff could be a problem, but of more concern were the drug connections and the vast network of organized drug distribution here. He did not know if they were looking for him, and he needed to make sure to not be seen. He needed to get in and out of this town and this area quickly.

Eastern Kentucky was coal country and was also one of the poorest areas in all the United States. Poverty was rampant, and the shacks and trailers in the hollers and low stream areas were filled with trash and tragedy. As Cal drove these roads, his eyes observed the children without shoes in winter. The lack of electricity in houses. The coal smoke from chimneys and stoves.

He rarely traveled to this area for work, even though Kentucky was part of his region. There was little need. His high-end kitchen equipment was not wanted or needed in this part of the state. He had been through once many years ago. He had seen the effects of low-cost illegal drugs, such as methamphetamine, on the small communities.

One of the few restaurant owners, a man named Garret, spoke to him about the situation. He had moved home to Eastern Kentucky after working in some great hotels and restaurants in the East. He inherited some land and a building on main street. He decided to create a regional and primarily southern style restaurant.

Garrett had explained it to Cal over drinks at his bar several years ago. He told Cal how methamphetamine was quickly becoming the number one threat to his home state of Kentucky, particularly in the rural areas of the state, his area. Meth production and distribution had increased frightfully over the last decade and spread like a wildfire. Mexican criminal groups were bringing in huge shipments to the area, and locals became the primary transporters and wholesale distributors of this Mexican produced methamphetamine.

However, not to be outdone, the locals were ramping up their own production over here in coal country where the mountains could hide many secrets. Soon, local production would exceed the imported varieties of the drugs.

He continued; it had become so bad recently, the local authorities had a backlog of open investigations and cleanup sites. Too many to handle. The hazardous chemicals were sitting there, and the producers were continuing to produce. These home-grown labs were dangerous and would occasionally explode, taking the men and women working them to a fiery death or a more gruesome chemically-induced death.

Local independent dealers and criminal groups dominated the distribution of meth in the state. In his own bar, he could see these pre-arranged drops and payoffs. It had become commonplace. Although the food was exceptional at his restaurant, this owner explained that without the bar doing a brisk business, he would go under. Garrett did not know how much longer his business would survive, but he was sure the drug business would be there long after he had closed his doors.

These once small and prosperous mining towns had suffered under the closing of many of the main street stores and restaurants. There was high unemployment and little to no opportunities for jobs, a career, or good wages outside of logging and coal mining. From what he had been hearing in the news, many of those jobs were now under attack, and companies had stalled out much of their operations in the region recently. The people here primarily relied on each other and the government's subsidies to survive.

He drove across the street to the gas station. He had been driving a long time and needed to fill his tank. When he was finished, he went inside to pay with cash. Standing on a metal rack near the cashier, with a good quarter inch of dust on it, was an old atlas for sale. He took it off the stand, shook the dust off, and tossed it on the counter. Then he turned around went down the aisle and grabbed some ibuprofen, Neosporin, and Band-Aids.

He walked back to the counter.

"Where are we in this thing?" he asked, pointing at the atlas. The local high school kid with big, bushy black hair and a nose ring grabbed the book. He started flipping the pages until he got to the state of Kentucky.

"We are right about here," he said. "Hyden, here is our road."

"Appreciate it. How much do I owe you?"

"$56.45," said the kid.

"Keep the change, thanks for the help," he said, and dropped three twenties.

"Thanks, man," said the kid.

He walked slowly back to his car, taking in the cool winter air while holding his side.

He needed to find his way back to the interstate, to a larger city. He needed a nurse to sew him up and some new clothes, but first he needed to find a television and get some more information.

All those needs pointed to Atlanta and Jennifer's house. He needed to check in anyway. If he left now, he could be there in less than six hours. Ben and Jennifer would know what to do, and what to make of all this new information.

He started the Jeep and drove out of town. He headed west toward the interstate and then to the Tennessee state line.

It had been only three weeks since he found the bags of cash in his yard. In a short amount of time, his life had changed dramatically. So many people were now dead, and how many more might die? It was time to get some answers and possibly get out of the country for a while. Hopefully, with the mayor and the two Springdale PD officers dead, the Springdale connections were gone. Should he risk returning and moving the money? Was there a better place to hide it right now?

Rule two, he thought. Don't lead people to the money until you know it is safe. Although the temptation was extraordinary to have the cash and hold it in his hand, he resisted the thought of returning home. Even though he would drive past his house soon on the way to Atlanta.

He was going to get some much-needed advice.

Chapter 23

"Do you think the mayor had the money the whole time?" asked Jimmy.

"I think we have what is left of it," Luis replied. "He may have laundered some of it for fifty cents on the dollar through one of his offshore companies. He did keep this cash back for some reason, or maybe he was planning on doing the rest later. Who knows?"

"What about this Wilson guy?" asked Jimmy.

"Boys did some research on him. He is a sales guy for a restaurant supply company. He took quite a beating from those Springdale pigs and was in the hospital. They said they visited his family in Atlanta, and he had been transferred to a recovery center in Arizona somewhere. We have no way to verify it, but it sounds legit."

"What do we do with him?" asked Jimmy. "Those cops were wanting the money so bad; I think they were chasing shadows. It sounds like wrong place, wrong time, and no idea where the money went, so let's beat the shit out of everyone."

Luis laughed. "They were in way over their heads from the start, but I do think their idea would have worked to rob us of the cash. They knew too much."

"That's for sure, we need to tighten up around here." Jimmy let out a sigh. "Make sure we have guys who are willing to take the fall, 'cause we take care of them and their families."

"We will be doing that for sure. I want info on all of us. Any outstanding warrants or anything the cops can use to flip."

"And this Wilson guy?" asked Jimmy.

"I still don't know, but something made them go after him."

"Yeah, they lost two million bucks and were desperate. Only a few houses to check. They probably broke into all the places."

"I think it was the mayor, you?" asked Jimmy again.

"I guess, but let's find this Wilson guy. We should have a talk with him."

"Beating him is not going to work," Jimmy responded. "The cops almost killed the guy and he told them nothing. If he does have the cash, he is not talking."

"If he even has the cash."

"Yeah, big if."

"We can still check it out, see if there is anything the cops missed. Two million is two million. We check him out."

"We got a lot of cash out of that vault," said Jimmy. "Glock estimates it at just over a million to one point two. The vault with about five hundred thousand in cash, plus the briefcase of a quarter million we got back."

"We did well on that deal. Plus, we needed to close up that fool. He was a big liability after we took out the cops."

"The collectibles and other trinkets are great for our business anyway. We will be able to trade them for product no problem. Did you see the price of that one little statue?"

"Twenty-five grand," said Luis.

"Yeah, and no questions from cops. This barter system will be great at getting us set up in Toronto."

"How?" asked Luis.

"We do not need to haul a bunch of cash across the border. We can take a couple moving trucks with furniture and household crap in it. Then we mix in the collectibles. No drug-sniffing dog is going to care about a twenty-five-thousand-dollar statue. Or a Mickey Mantle card from nineteen fifty-three. We can use them as a new currency or sell them to collectors for cash."

"I like it, have Glock sort it out. We can get clean cash by selling it on an online marketplace. We can use that cash for our new properties or for our rehabs. The stuff that is too expensive to sell online we will take with us. Start putting some trucks together, we fly out tomorrow," said Luis.

"You got it, Boss," replied Jimmy. "We can use the money in Florida, I have two more apartments to buy. We need about two million at closing."

"Not a problem. Did you move the cash into crypto?"

"Almost all of it. We have several guys in Atlanta buying it at those ATM machines and through some phone accounts. We should have it done by the end of the week."

Jimmy was walking around the desk. "Good, we will need to fly down to the Caymans and get all this sorted out in the next couple weeks. When is closing?"

"Three weeks."

"What kind of cash flow will this create?" asked Luis.

"This one has thirty-six units. Average rent is twelve hundred a month.

"Nice."

"That is roughly forty-three thousand a month before expenses and debt service," Jimmy responded.

"Listen to you, debt service," Luis said laughing.

"That's why you sent me to college," Jimmy replied.

"What does that take our total units and cash flow to?" asked Luis.

"One hundred seventy-seven units at an average of eleven twenty-five a unit is…" Jimmy was calculating the total on his phone.

Luis guessed, "Just short of two hundred thousand dollars?"

"$196,875."

"We have almost replaced the entire income of the gang," said Luis. "The difference is there is no risk and we don't have to use the money for security and more product. The profit margin is much higher."

"We should be able to run about sixty percent profit margin, making about one hundred and eighteen thousand a month," Jimmy answered.

"Very good. Let's keep rolling it over and buying more properties."

"If we can move what we have in the stash houses, we can buy two or three, plus whatever you find in Toronto."

"Good. Keep buying."

"Do we have anything else going on in Springdale right now?" asked Jimmy.

"Do you mean a yoga, drug, coffee shop?"

"I mean anything. We have closed out all our connections to Springdale. The marina thing is gonna bring heat our way. They had FBI, ATF, and our local gang units up there on site. They know they were TSG. They will be looking at us."

"I know."

"And?"

"And what?"

"Do you have any new plans for Springdale?" asked Jimmy with a bothered look on his face. He was starting to worry. He knew what this meant for the crews on the street trying to earn. Anytime the news covered a shootout or gangland shooting, the cops always put more pressure down on the gangs. The objective was to push every button, and hopefully, they would get lucky with a big drug bust or a capture of a wanted man. Their whole mission was a good news cycle for the cops, the city, and the politicians. The real crime would stay the same, but the appearance was the most important factor. After a while, everything would return to normal. However, it was hard to earn when your crews got busted or your stash houses got raided.

They were not heavy in product right now. They had twenty plus kilos of cocaine. Meth was running low, and a new shipment was supposed to be coming up from El Paso, but it was already behind schedule. They had probably a weeks' worth left. Meth was the new crack. Everyone wanted it, and it was easy to move. Inexpensive in the neighborhood and highly addictive.

In addition to everything else, the stash houses also contained about fifty pounds of weed. Some from California, some from Mexico. Most of it junk or dirt weed. They did not have the most demanding of clients. They wanted strong weed to get you high. That's what they had.

Luis was right; the best thing to do was to grind it up and put it into gummy bears, cookies, brownies, and anything else they could think of. Then sell it outside of their territory where no one was watching them.

"Springdale would be a great location for a satellite office," replied Luis.

"I know. Especially since those who would want a handout are gone. Seems to me you considered all of this already."

"In the coffee shop. It is a good place, the heat will be here, on us. Not there."

"What are we doing there?"

"Pedro will be in charge there. He is setting up some bakeries here to provide product. No storefront, but we will have some white kids head up there and get set up in a few weeks."

"None of our guys, right?" asked Jimmy.

"No, we stick out too much. No, we will just distribute."

"You sure it's not too hot there right now?"

"Jimmy, it is gonna get really hot here, and quick, not there. That is why we are leaving tomorrow."

"Tomorrow?" asked Jimmy.

"There is confusion in Toronto right now, and we need to be there to capitalize on it. We need to solidify our territory and take over the Russian operations now."

"How many men do we have there?" asked Jimmy. "Right now."

"Just over a hundred," came the reply.

"A hundred?" asked Jimmy. "How did you get a hundred in there?"

"Took about six months, but we got visas for some of the guys in Miami and Atlanta. They have been building a crew there under the radar. They have a small little territory in the Cuban district. It's working too. Making a little money, but that is not the goal."

"What is the goal?"

"Training, my friend. Training."

"How did you get weapons in Canada?" Jimmy asked laughing. "I know you can, but isn't it hard?"

"Yeah, man. I figured it out."

"Tell me."

"First, college boy, you tell me how you would do it," demanded Luis.

"Well." Jimmy paused for a moment and went over to the counter to grab a coffee. Jimmy did not offer opinions until he had thought out the possible pitfalls. This was a usual routine for Jimmy, and Luis was very understanding.

Jimmy filled two cups of coffee and walked back to the desk, placing one in front of Luis.

"*Gracias.*"

"Just off the top of my head, I guess I would avoid the sea. Too confined and too easy to be spotted on radar."

"Yes."

"If it were me, I would just dress up some guys and girls as hikers and fill their backpacks. Put them on a cross-border trail and have a car on the other side. A minivan and a mom with kids in the car."

"Great idea. But, no, I just drove them across. They are looking for drugs, not guns. Caches with guns and no drugs do not alert the dogs."

"Too simple!"

"It was."

"Why the big secret?" asked Jimmy.

"I planned this for a year to be perfect. I wanted to make sure the plan was ready to go. It had to look like an opportunity to move in and not my conquering of a territory."

"I understand."

"We will triple our income in a year, if we can hold it," said Luis. "Help me hold it, and let's put Pedro on Wilson, it's a two million recovery, after all. Tell Pedro there is a ten percent recovery fee."

Chapter 24

"Cal, please take back this money!" Jen blurted out at the dinner table after the kids had gone to bed.

She placed a grocery bag on the table. It was folded over many times and you could not see inside.

"Why?" Cal asked with confusion.

"One, you may need it, and two, it may put us in danger for having it. Thank you for thinking of us, and I know you did it out of a place of love, but this could be dangerous."

"Dangerous?" exclaimed Cal.

"Yes, what if the bills are marked or traceable somehow, I don't know."

"I doubt it, but if it put you in any danger, I would die, so I will take it," replied Cal.

Jen continued, "You may need it anyway. You can't get to the other money, right?"

"Not really, I think the house is being watched."

"What if you get home and something happens? What if you must run? You will need it then."

"True, thanks, sis. Always thinking of me."

"Do you have a plan if they come for you?" she asked.

"I have been thinking on it for a few weeks. Lots of time in the car to think."

"And?"

"And I have not worked it all out yet, but my thought is to get out of town. Just run."

"Agreed."

"Well, I will have to judge the situation," he added. "What if running puts me in more danger? What if I need to act like nothing is wrong? I know that is what kills everyone in the movies, but what if?"

"Don't be dumb, you run," added Ben.

"And he's a lawyer, you listen to him," Jen said.

"Alright, alright, I'll think about it."

Ben brought a pot of decaf coffee to the table in one hand and three mugs in the other.

"You think it is over?" asked Ben. "The cops are dead, the mayor too. It all seems so inside baseball."

"Well, the gangs are still out there, but the cops were obviously involved with them somehow. They were killed down here in one of their buildings."

"The cops did show up here looking for you," added Ben. "I don't think they would travel here just for a statement."

"So, they are the ones who…" Jen trailed off.

"Who kicked my ass?" asked Cal.

"Yeah."

"Looks like it."

"Well, they are dead, and you are alive," added Jen. "I think justice was served on that end."

"I am happy about it, no doubt," said Cal. "I don't have to look over my shoulder for the men in black. Now, I just need to see if anyone else is aware of me."

"If they are?" asked Ben.

"Plan B, run."

Jen looked up at Cal. "What's plan A?" she asked him.

Cal took a coffee mug and poured a cup of hot coffee. He sat back in his seat and thought.

"Do you need a minute on that one, big bro?" chimed Jen.

"Well. I'm terrible at this, obviously," said Cal. "I guess it's back to my original plan. I made some rules."

"Rules?" asked Ben.

"Yeah, you know, how not to get caught," said Cal.

"What are they?" asked Jen excitedly.

"Yeah, this I gotta hear," said Ben.

"Basic stuff from movies," replied Cal.

"Which are? Come on," prodded Jen.

"OK, rule number one is don't spend the money in public," said Cal. "Simple, right? Don't buy a Ferrari or fancy jewelry."

"Obvious." They both nodded.

"Rule two, don't return to the money until I know it is safe. I don't want to lead anyone to it or have it near me."

"Makes sense," said Jen. "I like that one. Not a fan of not spending the money one."

Ben and Cal had a good chuckle.

"I bet," said Ben.

"Hey," Jen snapped at Ben.

"Rule three," said Cal.

"Shhh," Ben said to Jen who was punching him in the shoulder.

"Got it, go easy on the bling," said Ben. "Next?"

"Rule three," Cal stated dramatically. "No unusual behavior. Go to work. Go home. Rinse and repeat. Act normal."

"And boring," said Jen.

"Yes, thank you, mom of four," laughed Cal. "Going to a lot of raves yourself?"

Jen punched Cal this time.

"I'll have you know we do not go anywhere," she replied with a tone of arrogance and sophistication.

"I need to go home," Cal said with a sigh. "What if these cops who died are the ones who attacked me?"

"It does make sense," said Ben.

"They were the only ones after me. They were the only ones who I ever had any contact with."

"But they are dead," said Jen. "That is not a good sign. I mean, if you were in the clear and no one knew anything about you, great. Those cops came to my door. They came to your door. Then somebody came for them."

"What is your point?" asked Cal.

"What if they told someone about you?" exclaimed Jen. "Or us."

"I guess we don't know," said Cal. "How would we know?"

"If they come for you again, or if people start coming by your place," said Jen. "That's how you know, and what if you get bound to a chair again?"

"Sis, I will not take chances. If I see something off, I'll run."

"Promise?" asked Jen.

"Yes."

"Is that all your rules?" asked Ben. "You can add run to it."

Cal looked up at his family who showed a real concern for him and his safety. They were right and he knew it. He had been on the run a while now, and he missed his little house, Daisy, and the simplicity of his life. He was good at hiding and getting lost. That was proven. He had new stitches and lots of bruises and wounds as proof of his criminal life. Was it criminal? Well, he had the wounds from his new abundant life.

He looked down at the table. "Ah, yes, one more rule. This was a late addition rule."

"What's that?" asked Ben.

"Rule four, see food, eat food."

Ben and Jen looked at eat other with a questioning stare.

"Eat?" asked Jen. "That is one of your big rules?"

"So many things happened to me around mealtimes. It prevented me from eating every time. I was so hungry."

The Browns both burst into laughter. Jen leaned back in her chair with her legs resting on the seat, her white pajama bottoms showing off their little pink unicorns. She slowly sipped her coffee and seemed to relax. Ben was drinking his coffee and staring at Jen.

These two were still in love after all the time together. Cal could see it every time he was with them.

"Oh, speaking of which," said Ben. "I have cake."

"Me, me, me," said Jen.

"Me too," said Cal.

"I knew you two would not pass this up."

"Where did you get it?" asked Jen.

"Break room."

"You're the man," she said.

Ben went out to his car to retrieve the cake.

"Can't leave it in the house with the kids?" asked Cal. "Little hypocrite."

"Ha, ha, very funny, but you don't have to be around the little boogers when they spike and fall. They are mean."

Ben returned holding what looked like a fancy baker's box. He opened it and placed it in front of them.

"Lemon Bundt cake," said Jen excitedly. "Score."

"It's a whole cake?" Cal said questioning.

"Oh yeah, it's fantastic. Everyone in the office is all anti-sugar, keto, low-carb, and so on. These cakes come from our vendors several times a year. A thank you gift."

"If he doesn't grab them, they get thrown away," said a giddy Jen. "Like the next day. Too big a temptation."

"Perfect," said Cal.

Ben handed them each a fork.

"Dig in," Ben said. "This is going in the trash after tonight."

"You guys are so mean to them," said Cal.

Cal pushed his fork down the side of the cake. Easing into the top, it glided down into the soft billowy and sticky layers.

With dramatic effect, he raised the fork up high and then down into his mouth.

"Oh my," said Cal.

"I know, right," said Ben. "These are like hundred-dollar cakes, such a waste on our department."

Jen had stopped talking and was enjoying her sugar. The room became very quiet for the next few minutes while they ate.

Eventually, they had their fill and finished the coffee.

It was time for bed, and Cal was heading out on Sunday morning.

Chapter 25

Pedro had a short conversation with Jimmy where he was told about the finder's fee for the recovered money. He was also told about Calvin Wilson, the mayor, and how it all connected. Pedro knew most of the facts but was now putting it all together. For two hundred grand, he would give it all a once-over at least.

Jimmy was holding a cup of coffee as they sat in one of Springdale's new high-end coffee shops.

"Let's get you some whitey clothes and a computer," Jimmy said. "After this, we are going shopping."

"Jimmy, man, stop it. Don't take this too far."

"It is my pleasure, don't worry about it."

"No, no, no, Rooftop said nothing about this."

"Lucky for me, I get to choose. College style, rich daddy, low ambition college grad, or tech guy?"

"Rich daddy? I'm Mexican!"

"Oh, we have rich ones, saw them in college."

"Really?"

"For real. Act like little white assholes."

"Well now, that just makes me proud," said Pedro laughing.

"When we are finished building our empire," Jimmy said, "your kids will have it too."

"Naw. I need kids first. Ones I know about."

"Well, when the payouts start, you will have to lock your doors to keep the ladies away."

"They can smell the money, can't they?"

"For sure."

"Where you gonna go, Jimmy? Some island somewhere?"

"I probably will never stop working on this. Problem is, guys in our business, we don't last too long."

"You right."

"The only reason we are still sitting here is Rooftop can see the future, the angles, and how to keep us out of trouble."

"And luck," said Pedro.

"Luck for sure."

Jimmy took another long sip of coffee. He set the paper cup down on the wood grain table and stared out the full-length front glass at the trees in the parking lot.

"Can you imagine being born here?" asked Jimmy.

"No, but I don't think it would matter."

"How you mean?"

"This little people here. Working for the paycheck. Big house. Big car. Big school bills. Big credit card bills. They are all working for the banks. They are prisoners in their own little world."

"Wow, P, that is deep."

"Yeah, I have thought about it. I watched some documentaries about the whole thing. These people almost killed themselves in 2008 when the economy crashed. Over what? A credit card statement?"

Jimmy and Pedro started laughing.

"Can you imagine one of us killing ourselves over money?" asked Jimmy.

"Never had it, not important. You can say a lot of things about our lives. It is dangerous, we have drugs, crime, and poverty, but we have freedom. We are not working for any damn banks."

"Social reformer."

"What?" asked Pedro.

"You, you understand something none of these people get. That makes you a social reformer if you try to change it."

"Naw, I will try to profit from it."

"That makes you a capitalist."

"Fine."

"Me too," said Jimmy.

"Now what?" asked Pedro.

"Your look will reflect your high intellectual ability." Jimmy was raising his cup to Pedro. "I will make you a computer programmer. No cop is gonna mess with your yuppy-looking ass."

"Great," said Pedro with a high dose of sarcasm.

"That is good news," explained Jimmy. "This way you get to wear expensive sneakers, not wingtips."

"What's a wingtip?" asked Pedro.

"Funeral shoes."

"Oh, they hurt."

"No shit. See what I did for you?"

"Yeah, thanks, I guess."

"Let's go shopping."

The two left the shop and made their way through the strip mall to the shops until the right jeans, shirts, and shoes had been purchased.

They left and made their way to the apartment community where the corporation had rented an apartment for Pedro, computer programmer. Next, they traveled to a local storage unit and rented two units. They looked at the map of available units and picked two that shared a wall. Pedro would enter through one unit always, but the unit behind it would never be entered through the door. He would cut a panel out of the wall and walk through to the other side. In that unit, items and boxes would be piled high so no one could get through the front. If the door was ever opened, it would look like a completely full unit. He would build the diversion at least two rows deep to make sure no light or eyeballs would make it through. Then behind that wall of junk he would hang some thick blankets from the ceiling, completing the illusion.

This would give Pedro an office away from everyone, including his crew. He would be able to store his product in here, and he would be able to store cash in the same way. However, Rooftop warned him about keeping the two items in the same place for more than a night. Jimmy agreed and so he rented another unit across town for the money, constructing the same elaborate camouflage.

Rooftop had always planned for the prying eyes of other gangs, or Feds. Pedro was a good soldier and did not cut corners. He followed Rooftop's instructions to the letter.

Within a week and a day, and after going to a storage auction, Pedro had completed both units. He had hired some movers to deliver the old dusty storage units to his new storage facilities, and then by himself he constructed the walls.

He was ready.

Jimmy came to inspect his work one afternoon and was impressed. It looked like it had been there for years.

They closed the front garage door of unit 312B and walked around to unit 212A for the last time. Jimmy gave Pedro three duffel bags full of baked goods and raw cut weed bags. Pedro went through the wall and placed the bakery items into the refrigerators in the back of the unit and stored the rest in a climate cabinet.

Now Pedro needed some young white kids to get his distribution done. He had met one at the coffee shop. A kid with a Bob Marley tee shirt and weed logo on his laptop. Pedro struck up a conversation with him. The kid, Caleb, told him he could get him some weed in about a week when his dealer came through town.

Pedro agreed. They hung out several times since. Pedro even bought him lunch at the Mexican restaurant.

Pedro bought the weed from Caleb. With that first drug buy, the trust between them was established and the relationship was born.

A week later, Pedro then explained the situation to Caleb. He was a computer programmer, but he had access to large amounts of baked goods, gummies, and weed. He needed a guy who he could trust. Caleb turned out to be his guy. He told him that he could make a lot of money distributing the stuff to his friends and the guys at his local college.

Pedro gave him some samples and told him to give them out. He could try one as well, but no more. Caleb agreed.

Three days later, Caleb called. He was in. His friends loved the stuff and he needed more.

Pedro set up the pricing model. Told him how much to sell it for and how much he purchased it for. The first round he would sell at a discount to build his cash flow. The next round was where he would start making money.

Caleb looked at the numbers and gave an enthusiastic yes to the proposal.

Pedro had his first distributor, but he was actively looking for three more. Rooftop was clear. Keep the distributors separate. They should not know each other and they should never meet.

Pedro found the Mexican restaurant a great place to transfer the product for cash. He bought five identical backpacks. He gave one to Caleb.

He explained they would meet at the back of the restaurant with the high wood booths with elaborate carvings. Both men would place their bags on the floor against the wall. They would kick them over to each other and then have lunch. Pedro explained there was a high degree of trust.

"If you are ever short on cash," explained Pedro, "you will be cut off. Period. The End. Done. No second chances. Understand?"

"I get it, man," agreed Caleb. "No second chances."

Pedro understood this privileged kid. He wanted Caleb to know he would put him out in the cold. He knew Caleb would not understand threats on his life or violence. This kid had not seen these things, and to him they did not seem real. Just made-up stuff in the movies.

Over the next week, Caleb made three drops at the El Ranchero Mexican Restaurant. Then Pedro dropped the new information on him. He was no longer going to be doing the drops. His friend Julio would now be his contact. Julio would know how to get in touch with him.

Caleb agreed, and the new contact info for Julio was exchanged.

The bags were kicked over, and Pedro was set up with his first distributor. He paid for lunch, grabbed his bag, and walked out of the restaurant. Outside, he broke his phone and threw it in the outside trash bin.

Julio would handle this from now on.

Pedro had another issue to handle. His mission now was to find two million dollars lost from the Russian deal gone bad. His goal was to follow all the families on the Windy Hill Road. Check around the exits. Build a map and a list.

First stop was Mr. Wilson. Why had the cops focused on him so much? They put him in the hospital and now he was in some recovery center out west. Most men break at the first sign of torture. He was either not a normal man or he knew nothing.

If he was not a normal man, then the allure of the money was more powerful than the pain he suffered.

He could understand this. He would not break under torture. For his family, his men, his crew, TSG, he would not break.

He drove his new company leased BMW SUV to the beginning of Windy Hill Road where it intersected with the main street road going through the town. He turned left and headed west toward the hills and mountains beyond. He drove slowly, taking it all in. First, he passed a grocery store and a Starbucks. He could see the road disappear behind the grocery store as it wound around a bend. He followed it. He could see the rolling hills in the road ahead. The terrain moved up and down and through more residential neighborhoods. New ones it looked like. Old farms and hayfields were on his right, downhill from the road which was following the spine of the ridge. On the left were trees, and for a while not many homes were visible. After a mile, Pedro could see a house on the right, smaller and older than the previous ones. Then a break and then another and so on. All in all, he counted eleven houses on this stretch of road. There were also neighborhood houses not facing the road but facing their new streets; however, the sides of the houses faced Windy Hill Road.

He discounted these. His friends would have looked for vacant land, vacant houses, or a ditch or disguised area to throw the money. Somewhere not easily seen from the road. Houses were a bad idea. Some of these houses were hard enough to see from the road and at night in the dark would be even harder.

Pedro reached the park and the marina. He turned around and made his way back. From this new angle he could not ascertain any new information. The bags could have been thrown anywhere and been fine for a while.

He knew the cops looked for them that night with spotlights and a slow search. They took their time. It was easy to determine the bags were not on this road at all. Or, a small chance existed that a neighbor pulled the bags out of their yard or field in the middle of the night, between midnight and four in the morning, before the cops finished their searching.

It all seemed too improbable. However, there was a lot of money out there somewhere. Pedro was betting on the mayor. He figured after he got the call from the cops, he set out on the hunt. He most likely found it, told no one, and then started to move it through his channels of money launderers, offshore banks, and hell, just buying stuff with cash.

The cops being found dead in Atlanta and the mayor's death were both creating a small media storm in Springdale. It was dying down now as the attention span of the public waned. Life was back to normal in the small town. People went to work, they went home, they shopped on Saturday and went to church on Sunday. Life continued.

Pedro was approaching Calvin's house. He pulled into the driveway and took a look around. This was one of the best places to dump the cash. There was a grove of pine trees and a ditch up by the road. It made it hard to see the house coming from the direction of the chase. But why next to a house? That made no sense.

Pedro got out of the BMW and walked to the front door. He knocked.

A voice from inside yelled out, "Just a minute."

Pedro could hear someone making their way toward the door.

"Can I help you?" asked Calvin.

"Yes, my name is Pedro Alvarez. I am doing some development in the area and I wondered if you had a few minutes to speak with me."

Calvin took a good look at the man. Hispanic, about five foot nine with short black hair he had plastered to his head with hair gel. He wore a blue sport coat, slacks, a white pullover shirt, and black with white striped tennis shoes.

He looked like he was right out of a magazine.

"What kind of development?" asked Calvin.

"Residential. I am trying to determine the ownership of some of the properties surrounding you. If I can acquire them, I am also interested in your property as well."

Pedro handed Calvin a business card he'd printed at the office supply store yesterday. He had made several business cards. One for a computer programmer role with Spectre Computing. Another one as an owner of Alvarez Development Corp. And one more as a security consultant with TSG Security Services.

All the numbers went to an internet phone number which he could forward to any burner phone.

"I don't know the owners of the farms around here." Calvin continued holding his side with the broken ribs, a habit he had to protect them. "The owners don't live around here anymore. They were gone, long before I moved in. Occasionally you will see kids and grandkids walking around, but mostly they lease the land to hay farmers."

"You alright? What happened to your side?"

"Yeah, I'm fine. I was in an accident. The ribs are broken."

"So sorry."

"It's all good, just tender. I am going back to work tomorrow. Been out for weeks. Insurance bills are crazy, and I really need to get some money coming in."

"Well, I may be interested in buying this place soon. Would you be interested in selling?"

"For the right price, sure. No low-ball offers. I know how many houses you can put on my little acreage."

"No low-ball offers," Pedro assured him.

To Pedro, Calvin at first looked fine. Then he could see him leaning against the doorframe and cradling his side. The face looked surprisingly good, but you could see the remnants of swelling and where it had been beaten. Calvin said he was in an accident. A way to move the conversation along. This man was brutalized and then sent back home to where it happened, and now he was being rushed back to work to be able to pay for the attack. Those cops were brutal and desperate.

"You have my card, reach out to me if you hear anything about the owners or any land around here that might be coming up for sale."

"No problem." Cal started to move inside the house.

"Have a good day," Pedro said.

Calvin waved in return and closed and locked the door.

Chapter 26

Calvin walked alongside his favorite chair and stood in front of the window. He watched as Pedro got in his BMW and pulled out of his driveway heading for town.

He held up the card in his hand. This did not seem right. Plus, this guy was Hispanic, like the TSG. Not being racist, but Cal was thinking about his wellbeing. He had to question everything now. He went to his computer, did a quick search, and found nothing on Pedro Alvarez or his development company.

"Oh, shit," he exclaimed.

He had always assumed someone was watching him, but they were definitely watching him now. The reality of it hit him like a fist in the gut. He sat back in his chair. Pressure built in his head and anxiety rushed through his body as his pulse rate rushed higher and higher. They were out there checking up on him. Making sure he did not have the money.

He had just got home. He was hoping that this was the end of the drama and no one else was out there.

It was time to get into the routine. He had to calm down and stick to the plan. He went to his bedroom and started packing his travel bag. He then went outside and began cleaning out his car. The camping supplies, food, and trash filled the back of his Jeep. He took most of it to his large city trash can, and the rest he put in the garage.

Cleaning up was soothing to Cal. Peaceful in fact. When he was done, he walked to the refrigerator and grabbed two long-neck beers and went outside. He sat down on the front porch and watched the road. No one was coming. But someone was probably watching him.

These were the times he missed Daisy the most.

If he was being watched, how could he ever spend any money? In reality, how could he ever move the money? Would it rot in the bags long before he could ever have the chance to spend it?

He was rich now. Rich in name only. He could not get to his money or spend it. If he did, the risk was too great of becoming poor, and most likely dead.

"Should I fake my own death, or should I just run?" Cal asked himself. He was so used to talking to Daisy, this habit was going to be with him for a while. He needed advice.

Cal picked up the phone and called his sister's house. After running down the scenario which just ended, the line was quiet.

"Brother, you should get out of there," said Jen.

"I agree," added Ben. "Get on the road."

"The last time, the cops came by in the morning; I was tied to a chair that night!"

"Run!" they both yelled into the phone.

Cal switched his burner phone to the other ear.

"If I run now, they will know," said Cal.

"So what, Cal?" begged Jen. "At least you will still be alive.

"Guys, I think I have an idea."

***

Cal was now driving to the Starbucks to get the strongest coffee he could buy. He was going for an exceedingly arduous drive and needed the caffeine. Screw rule number three. Time to run. He started up an audio book and hit the road.

Four hours later, Cal was passing through Macon, GA. He stopped at a large truck stop and filled the car with gas, but more important, he filled his belly with more coffee. He dipped into his large cash reserves to pay for everything. He needed to be sure no one was tracking his movements.

The deadline was tight. He needed to be there by eight in the morning at the latest. He still had a long drive ahead of him. According to his math, he had about two hours to spare.

After crossing the Florida line, he pulled off the interstate at the Florida Welcome Center. Not to get a tiny cup of Florida orange juice available to weary travelers entering the state, but to take a much-needed nap. He set his phone alarm clock for thirty minutes, reclined his seat, and was asleep in less than a minute. After a while, the alarm sound, radar, startled him awake.

"Can't be, too soon." He was groggy and tired. His mouth was dry, and his head was pounding. The pains of waking up tired. The car was chilly inside and the windshield had started to fog up. It was cool outside, but not cold.

Cal started the car and raised his seat. The audio book started back up where he left off. This crime drama had passed the time on the long drive south. Plus, the knowledge he was gaining regarding criminal activities was valuable to him. He was trying to glean as much information as possible.

"Just tell me how to launder the money!"

Screaming at the radio occasionally relieved his stress of this journey.

He merged back onto the interstate, headed for his destination. It was midnight, and according to the GPS, Cal had six hours to go.

When Cal finally parked the car in the long-term lot, he was exhausted. He saw the sign and, with his small travel suitcase in tow, walked to the window and purchased a one-way ticket. It was only twenty dollars extra for a premium ticket, so he agreed. He showed his passport, and he was off to the embarkation area.

He wheeled his suitcase down the dock and headed for the ferry.

This was Port Everglades, Florida, but soon he would be asleep on a ferry to Grand Bahama Island.

He had roughly fifty-eight thousand in cash on him now. He had regained the cash from Jen, the money he left for the kids' college fund. She felt it could have been numbered or tracked. Cal could not force her to keep it, so he added it to his bag. He would set up a fund for the kids one day when he could get to the money. His feelings about the house being monitored were valid. He knew he had to leave for a while. Let them get bored and forget about him and his little gray house. It was the only way. He had to get lost. Cal was now very tired, anxious, and feeling alive again.

The plan had been coming together in his mind for weeks. The first night sleeping in his Jeep, he asked himself the fateful question.

"Why don't the people in the movies just run?"

He asked himself more as a justification to what he was doing, but the idea had stuck with him. Running with all the money was not an option. Running on its own solved his problems.

In the horror films, why does the teenage girl run up the stairs to avoid the killer? In the dramas and thrillers, why do bad guys who are hunted by the US Marshals, and the entire police force, hide at their girlfriend's house? In the mobster movies, when you are going to a sit-down with the boss, why do you ride in the front seat of the car? If you are feeling threatened, why stay? Leave. These were the ideas moving through his conscience as he tried to sleep on his sore ribs.

Cal's darkest and greatest fear was being captured and tortured. So, his plan reflected that fear. He knew deep down in his gut he could not hold out again. It was dumb luck the first time. His body had not fully recovered from the initial beating. The thought of it brought back pain and anxiety. The stress was building.

He thought of the plan. Focus on the plan, he told himself.

The plan was simple. Get lost. They can't torture what they can't catch.

The house would still be there, and the goons could watch it forever, but his hunch was they would give up rather quickly. They probably knew he traveled for work. Catching him home and on the right day would require almost twenty-four-hour surveillance, maybe for the first couple weeks, but they would give up. Ben would pay the bills and forward the mail. Meanwhile, Cal was going on a long vacation. He hoped he could bounce around the Caribbean and South America for the next couple months. He could do it if he lived like a college student. He had friends who had gone a whole year bumming around the globe with little to no money. He had over fifty thousand dollars. He should be able to do it but with a little more style. He was over forty.

The plan was a bit limited after that. Eventually, he would come home and get the remainder of the money. Hopefully, the family land behind his property would stay in the family for the rest of the year. He was not going to be able to find out about it anytime soon.

It was a risk and he knew it. To Cal, at this point, the bigger risk was being caught, tied to a chair, and beaten, or worse. There was so much worse.

Besides, Cal was just excited to leave in the middle of the night, not to return for a long time. He had money, a small idea of a plan, and the adventure of a lifetime to begin.

The Bahamas was in front of him. Either way, he was getting to see sunshine and ocean, and a smile was on his face. The face of a crazy exhausted man, but he was smiling.

The saltwater air was blowing on his face, and the warm Florida sun was warming his body.

He was one of the last to board the ferry, and there were only a few people in line. He stumbled through and found a booth of chairs facing a table. He took the first one, stowed his suitcase next to him, and passed out in the upright chair.

The next sound Cal heard was an announcement of arrival several hours later. He was already feeling better and more alert. Luckily, the excitement was also kicking in. He had never been to the Bahamas and he was excited to see it.

First thing was first. A place to stay was the priority on the list. A lawyer was second. The bank was third.

Looking on his phone, he found a beach resort with a high rating and called to check availability. He made a reservation, explaining he was paying in cash. The desk clerk did not like it, but since things were slow right now, booked the room.

He made his way to the dock and found a cab.

"Bahama Beach Resorts, please."

"You got it, man."

"Thanks."

"You want air conditioning?" asked the driver.

"No, I want to smell the air."

"No problem."

Thirty minutes later, Cal was arriving in the large portico of a high-end beach resort. A valet opened his door, and Cal handed over the cash to the driver with a nice tip.

"Thank you, brother," came the reply.

Any cab driver who did not talk to him always got a good tip. He enjoyed the silence and observing the island.

"Any luggage, sir?" asked the valet.

"No, thank you, I'll take it."

Cal wheeled his small travel bag to the check-in desk and stood in line.

"Next, please."

Cal walked forward.

"I called in a reservation earlier. Last name is Wilson."

"Yes, here it is. First time staying with us?" asked the front desk girl.

"It is."

She went through the amenities and the dining schedule and then handed Cal some paperwork to sign. He gave her two nights' worth of cash, plus a one hundred and fifty dollar deposit.

"Here is your key."

"Thanks."

Cal made his way around the lobby. It was too early for the bar, and he was still tired. He found his way to the room and went to sleep.

Four hours later, he woke up starving and smelling like something had rotted. He took a shower, put on some clean clothes, and went down to the bar.

After ordering food and a beer, he started searching for small law offices on the island. He needed to incorporate a business and get a bank account. If he was going to be traveling, he needed one more layer of defense.

If he was lucky, he may be able to find a new identity. He was not holding out hope for that, but he would ask his new lawyer anyway.

After thirty minutes of searching and two beers, and some fish tacos, he was feeling much better. He placed a call to the law offices of Taylor Jones and Associates. He made an appointment for the next day at ten in the morning.

Cal had placed his money in the room safe but was worried about it and wanted to get it in the bank as soon as possible. This was his only lifeline for escape; without this money, running was impossible.

At the end of the bar, with a large hiking backpack on the ground next to her, sat a cute twenty-something with light brown hair pulled back in a ponytail. No makeup. She was wearing a tank top, brown shorts, noticeably short, and slim hiking shoes.

This was not the average look at this resort. Cal had been observing the ladies who looked like they spent an hour getting ready to go to the pool.

Cal left his seat and moved down next to the leggy brunette.

"Hi there," he said. "What's your story?"

She rolled her eyes at him. "Really."

"I am just wondering; you do not really seem to fit in with the forty-year-old moms in designer beachwear trying to hook up with the bartenders around here."

She laughed, a lot.

"You are funny. Yes. I am not here for that. Although, some of these ladies do know how to work it. Spend enough time here and you could learn a lot, I bet."

"I'm sure. Can I buy you a drink?"

"Why not?"

"I'm Cal, and you are?"

"Vela."

"Nice to meet you, Vela. Excuse me, bartender. Another beer for me and a…"

"Beer is fine," said Vela.

"You got it," replied the bartender. He pulled two from the cooler and popped off the caps, placing the two long-necks on the counter.

"Cheers," said Vela, and took a long pull.

"Cheers."

The two sat in silence for a long moment looking out at the ocean and drinking a frosty cold beer.

"So," Cal began. "Tell me what you are doing here. I am interested."

"Just passing through."

"Me too."

"Where are you headed?" Vela asked.

"I don't really know."

"OK, now I want to know your story."

"That's how I lure you in."

She laughed a soft and real laugh. She was smiling and turning her long tan legs in Cal's direction, facing him and wanting to know more.

"I am headed south. I think. I am going to take six months to a year and wander around," said Cal. "I was thinking about hopping through the Caribbean and then exploring South America. No real plan, just adventure. And you?"

"Same, but I have a plan."

"Really, where are you headed?" asked Cal.

"Bahamas to Haiti to Puerto Rico to Azures to Spain."

"Nice. Never been to Europe, but I have always wanted to go," Cal responded.

"So go, you don't have a plan," she retorted.

"True. I guess I am limiting myself again, even in my adventures."

"How do you mean?" she asked.

"We tend to put limitations on ourselves. I'd said I was taking six months to explore and find myself, but in doing so, I limited my travels to places close to my home. I guess. Don't listen to me."

"You're right. Exploration should be a long journey and to a place that excites you or you have a deep desire to experience."

"Where will you go in Spain?" asked Cal with interest.

"Everywhere."

"And then?"

"All of Europe. I am taking a long time off as well."

"How long?" asked Cal.

Vela grabbed the long-neck and took a long pull. She looked at Cal and smiled.

"As long as it takes, I guess."

"For?"

Vela looked out at the beach and a bleak look came across her face.

"Until I can find my own path, my own voice, and be at peace with myself."

"That is what we all search for, I guess."

"True, but I have been living a life of expectations for so long. I am finally breaking free. It took three years of law school and then passing my boards to determine that I may not like where my life is headed. I need to find myself before I can commit to the trap of my father and mother. Their father and mother, and so on."

Cal was terribly interested in this woman. She spoke as if she was truly a mature and learned individual, but she was young and beautiful. The concepts she discussed were middle-aged. He needed to spend more time with this beautiful creature.

"What is the trap?" he asked.

"Work is life."

"Indeed. It usually takes people fifteen or twenty years of the rat race to understand what you have already grasped. Congrats on law school and boards, but I agree with you. Live some life before you dig yourself into a work hole."

"Thanks."

"Are you independently wealthy?"

"No, my father is, but he cut me off because of my choices to leave and not join the firm right now."

"So, how long can you travel realistically?"

"I will go to a place, live, work, explore. Work some more until I can move on. This is my hope, at least."

"It sounds wonderful. I am guessing you don't have much money to spend, why stay here?"

"I'm not, just having a drink. I came on the ferry, and I always wanted to see this place."

They talked for an hour and were starting to get restless. Cal suggested they get a fresh beer and take a walk on the beach.

Vela excitedly agreed.

She left her backpack with the valet and got a claim ticket. Cal was going to offer to put it in his room for her but felt the insinuation was a little heavy. After all, he just met this girl.

Cal closed his tab and grabbed the long-necks and walked outside the automatic doors. A gust of warm air and the smell of the sea rushed into his face and overloaded his senses.

What a perfect day so far.

Vela was dipping her feet in a long fountain by the walkway.

She was beautiful in her simple clothing. Her mind was captivating, and Cal was captivated by her. She saw him approach and smiled.

This was going to be his life for a while, and for the first time in his life, he felt the fear and exhilaration of living life.

As they walked along the beach, Vela reached down and placed his hand in hers. They walked toward the setting sun, talking, laughing, and living. And, watching from the hotel bar was Pedro and one of his smartest lieutenants.

"Stay on him," Pedro said. "See if he leads us to the money."

THE END

Printed in Great Britain
by Amazon